The Deetkatoo

Native American Stories About Little People

The Deetkatoo

Native American Stories
About Little People

Edited by John Bierhorst

Illustrated by RON HILBERT COY

William Morrow and Company, Inc.

○ NEW YORK ○

Published by Morrow Junior Books
a division of William Morrow and Company, Inc.
1350 Avenue of the Americas, New York, NY 10019
www.williammorrow.com

Printed in the United States of America.
Book design by Jane Byers Bierhorst
The text was set in Mrs. Eaves designed by Zuzana Licko
10 9 8 7 6 5 4 3 2 1

Library of Congress Cataloging-in-Publication Data

The deetkatoo: Native American stories about little people
edited by John Bierhorst.
p. cm.
Includes bibliographical references.
ISBN 0-688-14837-9
1. Indians—Folklore. 2. Dwarfs—America.
3. Fairies—America. 4. Legends—America. I. Bierhorst, John.
E59.F6D44 1998 398.2'08997—dc21 97-29253 CIP

Permission acknowledgments:
"All Are My Friends." Adapted from A. L. Kroeber,
Yurok Myths, ed. Grace Buzaljko, by permission of the
University of California Press, copyright © 1976.
"The Rainmakers' Apprentice." Adapted from
William Madsen, *The Virgin's Children: Life in an Aztec
Village Today,* by permission of the author and the
University of Texas Press, copyright © 1960.
"The Talking Tree." Adapted from Ruth Warner Giddings,
Yaqui Myths and Legends, by permission of the University
of Arizona Press, copyright © 1968.

Frontispiece: "Anyone who goes to the river on a warm summer day
when the wind ripples the surface of the water—and listens
carefully—can hear the little people talking below."

Contents

Introduction

————

Little people are to be found in Native American folk-tales told in Canada, in the United States, and throughout the western hemisphere. Their appearances usually are brief, and the reader or listener catches only a glimpse of a half-hidden face, a miniature canoe, or a small helping hand. In some traditions the little people play a much larger role, as in the lore of the Cherokee of the eastern United States, probably the single richest source of American little-people tales. But stories in which the little people take center stage have been recorded from many other groups as well, including the Inuit of the far north, the Iroquois of New York, the Zuni of New Mexico, and the Toba of Argentina.

Although the stories are different from one region to the next, there is a sameness that cannot escape notice. Certain characteristics keep turning up, and it would seem that the little people have a style of life all their own whether they are imagined by the Inuit or the Cherokee, the Zuni or the Iroquois.

Their physical height at its upper limit is about four and a half feet, with two to four feet as the typical range (though some storytellers, fancifully, imagine them much smaller). The little people are wilderness dwellers seldom seen by average-sized humans. Yet, when visited, they prove to be generous hosts. They have inexhaustible food supplies, which they share or withhold as they see fit. They are capable of mischief, yet they can bring good luck. As small as children, they are wiser than adults. And though they are said to be old, even extremely old, they have great bodily strength.

In part, at least, these qualities suggest the folkloric little people of Europe. In the Grimms' fairy tale "Snow White," the seven little wilderness dwellers with their hospitable invitation—"Stay with us and you shall want for nothing"—offer much that could recommend them to a Native American audience. It might even seem that the idea of little people itself had been borrowed from the Old World. But there is no story quite like "Snow White" in Native American tradition, and in general the differences between the folkloric little people of Europe and America are as great as the similarities. Moreover, the Native little people have names all their own—*tlaloque, surem, deetkatoo*—and an American history that begins long before the Americas were colonized by Europe.

Rainmakers and Ancients

Diminutive human figures, different from average-proportioned adults, are well represented in Mexican and Central American archaeological collections. These date from as early as the Olmec civilization of southeastern Mexico, which flourished for about a thousand years beginning in 1200 B.C.

During the Classic period of the Maya, A.D. 300–900, the figures were sculpted on monuments and painted on clay pots. In some cases the little people that were depicted have labels in the ancient Maya hieroglyphic script reading *ch'at,* "dwarf."

It is not clear what stories or beliefs were attached to these figures. But in the folklore that began to be recorded in the 1500s, when Spanish missionaries had introduced the alphabetic script, two lines of thought emerge. One is that the little people are rain spirits. The other is that they are ancient inhabitants of the earth's surface, who long ago were either destroyed or driven underground. The two traditions are quite separate. Yet they have in common the idea that the little people live inside the earth, either in bodies of water and in mountain caves (in the case of the rain spirits) or in the underworld (in the case of the ancients).

In Aztec lore the little people were the helpers of the rain god, Tlaloc (TLA-lohk). Known as the *tlaloque* (tla-LOH-kay), these small spirits, together with their master, had power over rain and therefore controlled the food supply.

In one story the foods are said to have been discovered in mythic times when lightning struck Food Mountain and all the corn and beans that had been hidden inside it spilled out. The *tlaloque* stole the foods before anyone else could get to them and have owned them ever since.

Another story tells of a foolish king who played ball with the clever *tlaloque,* gambling away all his people's corn, including the crops they would plant in the future. The result was four years of hunger. Finally, when the people had nearly starved, fresh corn rose to the surface of a spring that poured from the rocks near the site of the Aztec capital. One of the *tlaloque* came out of the water and called to a passerby, "Hey, fellow! Do you recognize this?"

"O lord, I do indeed," said the man. "It's been a long time since we lost it." And with that the famine was over.

Though different from the *tlaloque,* the little ancients who lived on earth during the days of its creation were (like the *tlaloque*) superhumanly clever. Nevertheless they came to an end, so it is said, when the world was flooded or when the sun rose for the first time and scorched them. According to the Maya of Yucatán the great temples and pyramids still seen today were built by these original inhabitants of the earth, who worked in the ancient darkness before the sun was created. As evidence, modern Maya storytellers remind their listeners of the stone carvings of little people at the ruins of Chichén Itzá and Uxmal.

In some Mexican traditions the little ancients are said to have survived the flood by seeking refuge inside the earth, where they still live today. But because the sun passes through each night on its way back to the east, the underworld is unpleasantly hot. When it becomes unbearable, sometime in the future, the little people will return to the earth's surface, and the world as we know it will be entirely changed.

Since these stories can be traced to written documents that are earlier than the sources from any other region of the Americas, it is tempting to think of Mexico as the cradle of little-people lore. But how far the old Mexican traditions have actually traveled would be hard to determine. Certainly as far south as the Pipil of El Salvador, where the lore of the little rainmakers called *pipiltzitzin* (pee-peel-TZEE-tzeen) has a recognizably Aztec flavor. And probably as far north as the Yaqui of northwest Mexico and Arizona, where stories of the little underground *surem* recall the ancients of Maya tradition.

As far from Mexico as North Carolina and New York the basic ideas remain the same. The little people are rainmakers who control lightning and thunder. Or they live underground. Or they live in the water. They are said to have been on earth at the time of the Creation. And, most important, they have the power to provide food. But whether the stories about them have traveled from Mexico (undergoing great variation in names and details) or have been independently invented in many locales is a question that cannot be settled.

The Real World

Little people, of course, do not exist only in folklore. Extreme smallness of stature is a natural condition occurring in rare individuals, or dwarfs, in many human populations. If an entire community is of short stature, the term *pygmies* is used.

Some dwarfs, known to medical science as pituitary dwarfs, are small simply because the pituitary gland produces only a small amount of growth hormone. Most dwarfs, however, may be called *achondroplastic,* meaning that there is less connective tissue, or cartilage, between the bones than in average-sized people, which not only shortens the body but gives it different, more compact proportions. Pygmies may also have more compact proportions, but without achondroplasia.

Proving the truth of the old saying "In numbers there is strength," dwarfism has been regarded by Western culture as an abnormality; pygmyism has not. Native American attitudes on the subject would be less easy to characterize.

Interestingly, although a general rule cannot be given, the folktales in which little people enjoy the highest degree of respect—as among the Iroquois of New

York—are the stories told farthest from where natural little people can be found living in groups.

Real-life little people *in groups* are to be located only in two American regions: tropical South America and the Aztec-Maya area of Mexico and Guatemala. The South American groups, native to Colombia and Venezuela, are classed as true pygmies. The Aztec-Maya groups, known only historically, were achondroplastic little people assembled by kings to serve as court dwarfs; that is, as entertainers.

In the two regions, reality and folklore occasionally mingle. For example, along the Venezuela-Colombia border the Yupa tribe tell stories about the Pipintu, pygmies who live among the Yupa but maintain their own dwelling places and their own family groups. According to Yupa folklore, the Pipintu originally lived underground and became fully human only after intermarrying with the Yupa themselves.

Conversely, an old Aztec legend tells how a group of court dwarfs departed from the human community as their king led them through a snowy mountain pass. The king traveled on, but the dwarfs froze—recalling the Aztec *tlaloque,* or rain spirits, said to be mountain dwellers and, of course, sources of water.

In general, however, Native American folktales about

little people are entirely separate from the biological and social facts briefly sketched here. Evidently there is no connection in the storyteller's mind between the fictional tales and the known reality, at least not in most cases, and the little people are often envisioned in ways that contradict nature. Yet this does not mean that the subject is taken lightly.

Not Quite Folktales

Many, if not most, of the stories told about little people are said to be true. Moreover, these tales often have a matter-of-fact quality that suggests real-life experience. In some cases the tellers are simply reporting what they saw or what they believed they saw.

A typical example from a collection recorded recently among Cherokee people in North Carolina begins: "My mom's boyfriend says that his house is protected by the little people. One evening I was there by myself, and I could hear footsteps back in the hall. . . ."

Just as often the story takes the form of a secondhand report. The teller has not experienced the events but knows someone who has. "I have never seen the little people," begins an account from the same North Carolina collection, "but I remember my mother telling me some things. . . ."

Passed from mouth to mouth, such stories necessarily lose the element of personal recollection. Yet they are still told as true happenings. For example, another of the North Carolina little-people tales begins: "This man went out to hunt game for his family and got lost; you know, back then there were no roads or trails or anything, and it was easy to get lost. . . ." In this tale we no longer know the man's name or whose boyfriend or son he might have been, yet we feel that there might be someone who still does.

Though actively interested in stories of this nature, folklorists do not regard them as folktales in the ordinary sense. Such stories are called *memorates,* implying that they have been taken straight from memory despite their extraordinary subject matter. A memorate in its simplest form is no more than a direct account of someone's experience with the supernatural.

Told again and again, if it is truly memorable, the memorate begins to acquire the trappings of the storyteller's art: a faraway locale, an ancient time frame, a well-developed plot with a satisfying ending, and perhaps even a moral.

The stories in this book, for the most part, are in

between the memorate and the true folktale. It may be said that they are on their way to becoming folktales. Many are quite short, with abrupt endings. They may lack the carefully worked out situations that we expect when reading or hearing other kinds of folklore. Yet this shortcoming is their virtue. These stories have an immediacy that places them in a category distinct from fiction. Having not quite lost the sense of firsthand experience, they are capable of putting us in touch with deeply held beliefs that come to the surface naturally and blend with everyday life.

Sources of Power

For the Inuit of the Arctic regions the folkloric little people, traditionally, were among the many kinds of beings that could serve as guardian spirits. Each person had a particular spirit helper that might come to the rescue in time of need.

Typically, the person would recite the words of a short charm, or formula, in order to "call" the helper to come cure disease, bring game animals, quiet a storm, or overcome an enemy. In the Inuit story "Two Bad Friends," a young man who has the little people as his guardians calls out to them to save him from drowning.

Little people have also been regarded as a source of personal power among the Cherokee of North Carolina and Oklahoma, and charms were formerly recited to secure their aid. In some cases the one in need would identify with the little helper, using the words "I am to fail in nothing! I am a Little Man." Or, seeking protection, the user could call out to the helper, "You will be holding my soul in your clenched hand!"

Among the Seneca, the westernmost of the Iroquois nations of New York, the little people, or *djokáonh* (jo-KAY-oh), are called upon not privately by individuals but by a gathering of singers and dancers who meet indoors after nightfall to perform what is known as the Dark Dance. According to one description, the ritual consists of 102 songs in four sections (of 15, 23, 30, and 34 songs). It is said that the "little folk" themselves enter the darkened room and join in the singing, bringing with them the power to cure sickness. The origin of the ceremony is explained in the story "How the Dark Dance Began."

Another group ritual, addressed to the spirits called "little old ones," is performed every several years by the Nahua, or modern Aztec, of east central Mexico. The little spirits are said to be a company of twelve. They dress in black, the color of rain clouds, and they carry walking sticks. From a cave near the summit of a certain mountain, so it is said, they issue forth to distribute rain. Therefore the ritualists make a pilgrimage to the mountain cave, carrying walking sticks like those used by the "little ones," to appeal for the rain that is needed to water the farmers' fields. These modern Aztec *tlaloque,* or rain spirits, are known in various parts of central Mexico. "The Rainmakers' Apprentice" is one of the stories told about them.

Little people who are also rain spirits, or thunder spirits, are known not only to the Nahua but to the Iroquois and the Cherokee. The Iroquois thunderer is *Hinon* (HEE-noh), said to be a little man between four and five feet tall.

Hinon is not related to the little people who come to the Iroquois Dark Dance or who occasionally pop out of the woods and surprise travelers. But in Cherokee lore the "thunders," sometimes regarded as twin brothers, do belong to the company of little people and have family ties with them.

Among the Zuni of New Mexico there is no general little-people lore, yet there are two little brothers, called *Ahayuta* (AH-hah-YOO-tah), said to live on Corn Mountain, also called Thunder Mountain. According to one story these two "little ones" stole lightning and thunder and caused a storm that still has repercussions in the Corn Mountain area, where lightning displays and rain showers are said to be frequent.

In most stories the Ahayuta are tricksters. But unlike the well-known Native American tricksters Raven and Coyote, who are typically foolish and incompetent, the Ahayuta play to win and are generally successful. In "The Little Ones and Their Mouse Helpers," for instance, the brothers are confronted with the impossible task of doing a year's work in one night. They meet the challenge by enlisting an army of mice to do the work for them and win a bride as a reward for their cleverness.

But the Ahayuta are more than tricksters. They are also war gods, who protect the Zuni people. Represented by wooden statues two to three feet high, the little war gods receive prayers and ritual offerings of cornmeal and turquoise in exchange for the blessings of safety and good health. Two new statues representing them are carved each year and placed in outdoor shrines.

Since the late 1800s and until recently, the carved

wooden Ahayuta were sought by souvenir hunters and art collectors, and many were stolen from their shrines. In the 1970s a single statue could bring as much as $40,000 on the art market. But in 1978 the Zuni began quietly approaching museums and private collectors, explaining the importance of the Ahayuta to the Zuni people and asking for their return. So persuasive was the appeal that as of 1996, eighty-five of the "little ones" from collections all over North America had been returned to the Zuni.

○ ──────────────────────────────── ○

The strength and wisdom of the little people, in defiance of their small stature, add believability to the idea that the powerless can be made powerful. The message behind the stories is that anything is possible. Regardless of how weak or how small one may be, there is no gift, no power, that cannot be acquired—the power to withstand disease, to find food, to control the weather, to triumph over enemies, and, above all, the sheer power to endure.

It is believed that when the Cherokee were forcibly removed from Georgia in 1838–39 and set out for Oklahoma on the Trail of Tears, the little people comforted them along the way. It was they who protected the Everlasting Fire from rain and snow during the long journey, and when the Cherokee arrived in northeastern Oklahoma, the fire, which had been painstakingly brought from Georgia, was entrusted to them. It still burns today because the little people, so it is said, are tending it.

In Cherokee lore the little people have been called "the eternal ones," and tradition states that they were present when the world was being created. Similarly, an Iroquois account mentions that one of the little people was the first person to be seen after the world had been made, and, as affirmed in the Passamaquoddy lore of eastern Maine, the *oonabgemesuk,* or little people, were indeed the "first born" on earth. The same is true of the Yaqui *surem* of northern Mexico, who were alive on earth before the Yaqui themselves, and who remain underground today as a source of power for Yaqui people, as told in the story "The Talking Tree."

Time may run out for ordinary mortals, but not for the little people. As expressed in a modern belief of the Tzotzil Maya of southern Mexico, when the year 2000 arrives the world will flip over and the little people, who have been underground since the days of Creation, will once again be on top.

The Deetkatoo

Native American Stories About Little People

Weaker and Weaker

Inuit BAFFIN ISLAND

It was long ago, and the old people's children grew up and had children, and their children's children had children, and their children's children's children had children, until the island they lived on filled up with people, and one day it tipped into the sea. Everybody was washed away except one grandmother and her grandson.

"And what will we do now?" said the grandmother. "We must make ourselves strong." Then she began to sing:

> my teeth are flint
> my stomach is copper
> my heart is a hammer

But it was no use. Every day the grandmother and her grandson grew weaker.

At night they would crawl into the one house that was left on the island and try to stay warm in a small room to one side of the main room. With no oil for their lamp, they went to bed early, always hungry. They were getting weaker and weaker.

One evening when they had lain down in the dark and the little boy, as usual, had said, "I wish some living thing would come"—and nothing had come, not even a rabbit—they heard a noise outside the passageway.

A very small man and his wife were just pulling up with their sled. They came to a stop right at the door, and seeing no light, they said to themselves, "The house is empty."

They unloaded the bags of walrus meat they had brought on their sled and set them in the passageway. Then they went into the main room of the house and made their beds, and as no one said to them, "Don't come here," they lay down to sleep.

The grandmother could hear the talking of little people, and as soon as the house had become quiet again she said to her grandson, "Go into the pas-

sageway where they put their meat. Touch your finger to your tongue, then draw your finger around the bottom of one of those bags, touching both the bag and the ground."

The boy did exactly as he was told, then crawled back to his grandmother.

When the dawn came, the little people were up again and about to go on their way. While the little husband was getting the sled ready, the little wife was taking the meat out of the passageway. But one of the bags was so heavy that when she tried to lift it she could not. She shouted to her husband, "Yesterday it wasn't heavy at all. Now I can't move it."

The little man jumped from the sled and tried to lift the bag. But it stuck to the ground. He tried again, and still it stuck. He called into the house, "Then take it!" and as they sped away he said to his wife, "I *thought* there was somebody there."

After that the grandmother and her grandson had good times and were cheered up for a while. They had plenty of food. They weren't hungry. And here ends the story. Now sleep!

Three Wishes

Here's my story. Long ago there lived a family that was always happy, never hungry. The father was a good hunter, and the mother was a good cook.

In this family there were four children. One of them was a daughter who was brave and liked to go places, and many times she would go by herself and sit near the river, far from home. There she would think about all sorts of things, good things that might come to her family. This daughter's name was Gathering Flowers.

One time, as she sat by the river, she fell asleep, and in her sleep she heard talking. She awoke and sat up, and there in front of her was a family of little people walking along, a little man, a little woman, and three tiny children. The baby of the family was on a tiny cradleboard.

Gathering Flowers's mother had often told the children stories about the little people, saying, "If you ever see them, don't be afraid. Talk to them, be nice to them, and they will bring you luck."

Remembering what her mother had said, she was not frightened at all. She spoke to them: "Come here, sit down and rest. You must be hungry. I have corn bread and apples. Have some." She also gave them cool water to drink.

"Where do you live?" she asked.

"Over there on the hill," they answered. "Will you come for a visit?"

"Yes," she said, and she began to follow them.

After a while they came to a small rock, and the little man spit on his hands, put them against the rock, and rubbed it. Suddenly the rock split open and the little family went right through the crack and into their house.

"I can't get through this tiny opening," said Gathering Flowers.

"Oh yes," said the little man. "I forgot you are bigger than we are."

He spit on his hands, reached up to her, and

rubbed her head. Suddenly she felt herself getting smaller, and in a moment she was the same size as the little people and was able to get through the opening in the rock.

Inside the house was a tiny table. And there were chairs, beds, and a stove with a pot of soup. Gathering Flowers was invited to sit down and have soup with the little family. The mother kept taking more soup from the pot, but no matter how much she took, the pot was always full.

When it was time for Gathering Flowers to go home, she went through the narrow opening in the rock, and the little man followed her. He spit on his hands, touched her head, and suddenly she grew back to the size she had been before.

"Promise you will not tell anyone you have seen us or where we live," said the little man. She gave her promise, and after that she visited the little people whenever she liked, all summer long.

When autumn came, it was time for Gathering Flowers and her family to move to her father's hunting ground. Once more she went to visit her friends, this time to tell them good-bye.

The little man saw that she was a good person and said, "Because you have been kind to us and have kept our secret, I will give you three wishes.''

And for her first one, here's what she chose: ''I wish for a magic soup pot so my family will never be hungry and we can always give soup to strangers who pass by.''

And here was her second: ''I wish for the wisdom never to hurt anyone with words that come out of my mouth.''

And her third was this: ''I wish to be able to see something good in everyone I meet, not just their faults.''

''You have made wise choices,'' said the little man. ''You will be happy for the rest of your life and your luck will always be good.''

Proud-Woman and
All-Kinds-of-Trees

Seneca NEW YORK

There was once a young man who tried to have better luck by taking medicine. He would take it for ten days before leaving the village to go hunting, and the medicine he used was made from the bark of all kinds of trees.

But even with medicine his luck was bad, and for this reason he would carry a load of parched corn to keep himself from starving if he found nothing.

Now, on the outskirts of the same village there lived a mother and her daughter, whose lodge the young man had to pass whenever he started out on a hunting trip, and one day when he passed, the daughter shrugged her shoulders and said,

"Hu-hu! There goes the hunter who gets nothing."

She turned to her mother and said scornfully, "Look who just passed: All-Kinds-of-Trees."

But the thrifty mother, who desired a good match for her daughter, spoke sharply: "Why do you make fun of him? He is a good man, the best in this village. He keeps on hunting, and one day his luck will change. I wish he were your husband."

The young woman answered, "If you say so, I can go with him." Then in great haste they made the marriage bread, and when twenty loaves were ready the daughter placed them in her pack basket and followed the trail of the young man. When night overtook her, she lay down to rest on a mossy rock.

Just as she was falling asleep, she heard the footsteps of someone approaching. The sounds were *deet, deet, deet, deet, deet.*

In a moment a little man of the woods came up to her, laughing, and said, "Ha ha! Here's Proud-Woman, following the trail of a very poor hunter. Go, go on! He's waiting for you." Then he shook her and teased her. "Go!" he said. "All-Kinds-

of-Trees is waiting for you. Just over there!"
Again he teased her. "Proud-Woman!" he cried,
and he shook her with his little hands. But he
could not shame her. When daylight came, he said
to her at last, "You are free." Then he ran away.

After making a cold bite do for breakfast, the
young woman took up the trail again. Just as she
had been told, she found the camp of the hunter
not far from the spot where she had slept the night
before. The young man, hearing her breathe,
looked up. She smiled and handed him the basket.

"Here is marriage bread," she said. "I have
come to marry you." He thanked her and ate the
bread.

And so it is that a man and a woman decide to
stay together and whisper together and love one
another and be happy. Then for two changes of
the moon they camped in this spot.

But when the twenty loaves had been eaten and
even the parched corn was gone, the young hunter
said to his wife, "If I have nothing to eat tomorrow, I may not be able to get up."

That day while hunting he saw a small lodge, and
he said to himself, "How strange it is that I have
never noticed this little lodge before."

Peering in through the doorway, he saw a little woman, who welcomed him and gave him a bowl of green-corn soup. While he was drinking the soup, he saw a tiny baby on its cradleboard next to the fireplace. It was so beautiful he could not keep himself from reaching into the lodge and picking it up. Then, without thinking, he tucked the little child into his shirt and ran off. The little woman was chasing behind him.

Immediately the trees began to moan. The sound grew louder, and a storm blew up. Wind tore into the forest, sending bushes and trees through the air in every direction. "I will be dead any moment," thought the hunter.

Suddenly, as he ran past a fallen tree, the little man of the woods jumped up and stood on the tree trunk, calling out, "Did you steal my baby?"

"Yes," said the hunter. "I stole it because I had never before seen anything so pretty."

"Give it back," said the little man, "and promise never to do it again. In return I will make you the greatest of all hunters."

"Here, take it!" said the hunter, and he handed the tiny child to its father. "And I will never do it again."

"Then we are of one mind," said the little man. "We have made the agreement strong. From now on we will call each other 'friend.' " As he said the words, he carefully unwrapped the baby and, taking a tiny arrow from the child's wrappings, gave it to the hunter.

"This is yours," he said. "It will bring you luck."

All at once the storm stopped and the wind calmed down. Then the hunter found his wife again, and together they returned to their village. From that time on, the man found game whenever he hunted. His wife was heard to say, "We can live now; we have plenty," and before long the two had a child of their own.

For the rest of his life the hunter was always successful, and it was said by those who knew what had happened that his luck came from the friendship of the little man of the woods.

The Girl Who
Married the Little Man

Inuit GREENLAND

There was once an old couple who had a daughter, and in the village where they lived there were many men who were thinking of marrying her. The parents, however, wished otherwise and made every effort to keep their daughter at home.

One man in particular was eager for marriage. He came repeatedly, and at last he fought with the old father and nearly overpowered him. Running swiftly, the old man got to his boat, managed to load it, and narrowly escaped with his wife, his daughter, and all their belongings.

As they were pulling away, the rejected man and all the other men of the village shouted after them contemptuously: "It won't be easy now for you to get a husband for your daughter," "The poor thing can't hunt," "How dare you reject us," "Just wait until you're hungry, then see if there's anyone to help you."

But the old man kept paddling, without bothering to answer, and after a while the family landed on one of the outermost islands. There they built a new house and put up for the winter.

One morning the old man awoke, saying, "What have I just seen? Was that a man gliding through the doorway?" He questioned his daughter, and as she kept silent he grew suspicious.

When he awoke the next morning he saw the same thing more clearly, a small, stout man slipping out the door. On being questioned, the daughter confessed. "Yes," she said finally, "I am married to one of the little people."

Hearing this, the father thought for a moment and was happy. Then the daughter went on, saying, "My husband is afraid you won't like him, so he keeps out of sight. But if you don't mind, he will come live with us."

The next morning, opening his eyes, the old man turned toward the entrance and saw nothing unusual. Then, turning around to his daughter's resting place, he saw the little man sitting beneath the daughter's lamp.

The father was well pleased and leaned back on his sleeping platform. But when he listened again and looked, the little man was no longer there.

Toward evening the daughter left the room. When she returned, she had a hunting line, which she hung on a nail to dry. She turned to her parents and told them her husband had come back from hunting and had brought his catch, but now he had gone off again to take meat to his relatives.

Rushing outside to have a look, the old parents found many freshly killed seals on the beach and rejoiced to see that they were suddenly rich.

The following morning the old man peeped over the screen that separated him from his daughter's resting place, and there was the son-in-law, as before. In a little while, however, the old man heard someone stirring, and by the time he got up, the son-in-law was already out the door.

Again the old man spoke to his daughter: "Why don't you tell him to spend time with us? We like him very much."

That evening, when the little man returned with

his catch, he stepped inside and at last made himself at home. The parents were as friendly as they could be, and the family lived happily through the rest of the winter.

When spring came, the son-in-law announced that they would soon be traveling to new hunting grounds for caribou. But first, he said, he would have to visit his own parents. Since he was their only son, he had to provide for them, and for his sisters, too. Then he left for his old home. When he returned, it was time to start toward the caribou grounds.

The old father put everything into the boat, and when it was loaded and they were ready to set off, another boat suddenly appeared, shooting straight out from the beach. Who was it? It was the little man's relatives, come to guide them.

The two boats went along together and landed at the same time that evening. Next morning they started again. When they came in sight of an unfriendly village, the boat full of little people pulled out in front, and their headman called back to the other boat, "Keep close!" All of a sudden the two boats dived downward and were paddling beneath the waves. Safely past the unfriendly village, they rose back to the surface and kept going without danger.

Reaching their destination, they made camp for the summer, and the little son-in-law went caribou hunting. When it was time to leave, they piled the boat high with furs and meat. The son-in-law had provided for them plentifully, and on returning to their winter quarters they were comfortable and well off.

About this time, news came that the men who had once scorned the old father and his family were now at the point of starvation. Immediately the father set off for the mainland, and before long he returned with all the men who at one time had wished to marry his daughter. They came in a long train of kayaks. When they landed, they were treated very hospitably, and the little son-in-law and his wife served them caribou and seal meat.

When the dishes had been set before the guests, the old man said to them in a loud voice, "I wonder if you can still remember what you were telling me a long time ago, when you had nearly killed me, trying to steal my daughter. Can you remember? Your words were these: 'You will surely never

get a clever son-in-law.' But in spite of your insults you see what I have. And you said you would never help me if I came to you hungry. Now, please, help yourselves, and eat as much as you like."

And that's the story.

The Little Ones
and Their Mouse Helpers

Zuni NEW MEXICO

A tale of the ancient days, long ago. There were
people at Yellow Rock Village, and in the house
with the tallest ladder lived the village priest and
his only daughter.

From birth the priest's daughter had been given
the power to hunt, and whatever animal she wished
for she could easily find, so that her father's house
was filled with meat. Handsome young men from
the seven towns came asking to marry her, but she
sent them all away.

In those days two little ones, two not-to-be-
thought-of-as-great-men, were living at Thunder
Mountain with their grandmother. Having passed

through the village many times, they announced, "We have seen the priest's daughter and we think of her all day long."

"Ha!" said their grandmother. "You are not handsome. You are too small, you will be laughed at."

"Ha!" said the two little brothers, and the older one said to the younger, "When I look at you, you are handsome." The younger one said to the older, "When I look at you, you are extremely handsome," and when the sun had almost set, they called out to each other, "Let's go."

Arriving at the house with the tallest ladder, they climbed up quickly, giving a shake, and the bells on the topmost rung began to tinkle. People inside said, "Someone is coming."

"We come!" said the little ones, and they tumbled into the room. The old father greeted them, while the daughter brought wafer bread, deer stew, and meat broth to drink.

When the little guests had eaten, they said to the father, "We come with thoughts of your daughter."

Then the father turned to the young woman, and the young woman turned to the guests. "Which one?" she asked.

"Take us both," said the younger brother.

The daughter said nothing at first. Then she led the little ones into another room and said, "Rest here. You are not yet my husbands. I will test you in the morning."

When she had gone, the two little brothers laid their arms across their eyes and slept until the dark disappeared and the sky was just turning yellow.

As they sat up, the young woman came into the room and said, "You must prove to me that you can dress deerskins. For a long time deerskins have been piling up in the room above. I have no brothers to soften and scrape them. Take all the hair off by tomorrow at sunrise and scrape the undersides so that they will be thin and soft, and I will agree to be your wife."

But when the brothers were shown into the upper room, they said to each other, "How can we scrape so many? There are more than can be cleaned in a year." The deerskins were packed to the rafters.

Not knowing what else to do, they heaped the skins into bales and carried them to the river. They made a dam so the skins wouldn't float away. Then they laid them in the water to soak overnight.

As they worked, they heard sounds of talking from the hill on the far side of the stream. In the ancient time this hill was the home of the field mice, as it is today. But in those days the mice were great gamblers. They were always betting away their nests, and since they had growing families, they were constantly in need of hair to make more and more nests.

Following the sounds of the tiny voices, the two little brothers crossed the river and climbed to the top of the hill. "Let's go in," said the younger brother, and as they crawled through the hole, a voice said, "Who comes?"

"We come!" they answered.

"Then come in!" cried the mice, but they kept up their shouting and calling out to each other. Many had gambled away their nests, and some were starting to bet their clothes.

"We heard voices," said the brothers. Then they told their story.

"What?" cried the mice.

And the brothers repeated what they had just said: "We must clean all the hair off those skins by tomorrow." Suddenly the mice stopped shouting and looked around at one another. Their eyes were sparkling.

"We will help you," they said, "if you promise to give us the hair."

"Oh yes," said the little brothers. "We will be glad to get rid of it."

Then all the mice began pouring out of the hill like water when rain falling hard runs over the rocks.

Finally, when the last one was out, the two little brothers pulled the deerskins onto the bank, and the mice started nibbling the hair and cleaning off the undersides. They made little bundles of the dried bits of meat to save for food and large packs of hair to make their nests.

All night they worked, and in the morning the two little brothers gathered up the skins and spread them on the sand. When the priest's daughter arrived, there were the skins, all soft and white, stretched out in front of her like a field of snow. She was overwhelmed.

She looked and looked. Then she got a long pole and fished in the water, but no skins were there. She counted and recounted. Every skin was on the sand.

"Your power is greater than mine," she said finally. "You will be my husbands. I cannot say no."

Then she took the two little ones back to her house, and they all lived together from that time on. With the meat that the young woman got from her hunting, and with all the soft skins anyone could ever want, they managed to get along comfortably. And, it is said, they never quarreled. Well, this happened a long time ago.

And that is the end.

All Are My Friends

Yurok CALIFORNIA

At the end of the sky a boy grew. He thought, "I wish to know the world. I want someone to talk to me." Then he changed his mind and thought, "I'd better sleep. I think I'll dream." He lay down.

Before he slept, he noticed a little stick. Then, as he slept, he touched the stick, and in his dream he saw the stick move, get up, and turn into a small man.

The little man spoke: "Boy! Don't you know me?"

"No, I don't know you."

"Well, look at me, so you will know me."

The boy looked. The little man was carrying a

sack on his back, but the boy saw no pack strap or cords across his breast. Instead he saw holes through the little man's shoulders, and cords in the holes. The sack itself was made of netting.

The little man said, "You mustn't say, 'How did he come to look like that?'—because I never take it off. I grew that way. I'll let you know my name. My name is Megwomets. In this world you will see many people. All are my friends. I keep food for them and give them everything they need to eat. Look into my sack."

The boy looked. He saw salmon, eels, acorns, all kinds of seeds, berries. Everything good to eat was in the sack.

"I carry these seeds for my friends," said the little man. "I take them and throw them everywhere, and they grow for my friends. I do the same with salmon and eels. I throw them, and they jump in the water for my friends to catch. That's the kind of person I am. Now go around the world, and you will get to know the land. Go down to the river and catch salmon. Go uphill in autumn and you will find many acorns."

The boy awoke. He heard a bird singing.

And from that time on, if people were hungry,

the voice of Megwomets could be heard, saying, "How are my friends?" And if the answer was "Oh, they are poor—food is hard to get," then Megwomets would throw food.

"How are my friends?" he would ask again. "Do they have enough?"

"Yes," the people would say, "we are eating acorns. We have enough."

And the little man would always answer, "That is good!"

The Little House
in the Deep Water

―――――

Cherokee NORTH CAROLINA

In the old times when the animals used to talk and hold councils, there was a year when the bear, the deer, and even the squirrels decided to make themselves scarce, so that hunters who went to the woods came home empty-handed and even the children had to go out and hunt for food.

One day a boy who had been tramping over the mountains without finding any game sat down on a log to rest, wondering what he should do. Suddenly he felt a stone hitting him in the shoulder. He looked to the ground, but no stone had dropped. He looked up again, and there was a little man all dressed in white, with hair that fell to his heels.

"Come take a walk up the river," said the little man.

"No," said the boy, "I have to go home to dinner soon."

"Come right to my house," said the stranger. "I'll give you a good dinner and bring you home again in the morning." So the boy began to follow him.

The little man led the way along a trail through the woods that the boy had never noticed before. When they came to a creek, the little man stepped into the water and kept going. The boy stood back in surprise. He thought to himself, "He's walking in water. I can't do that."

"He's-walking-in-water-I-can't-do-that," said the little man, for the little people talk the thoughts of others without their saying a word. Then he turned to the boy and said, "It's not really water, it's only the road to our house."

Still the boy stood back. He was afraid. But the little man led him by the hand, and when he finally stepped into the water, it was just soft grass, and it made a trail.

They followed the trail until they came to a river. The little man plunged in. But again the boy stood back, thinking, "That water is very deep and will drown me. I can't go on."

"Drown-me-I-can't-go-on," said the little man out loud. But then he said, "This is not water. It's just the main trail to our house. We're very close now."

The boy stepped in, and instead of water there was tall waving grass that closed over his head as he followed in the footsteps of the little man. When they came to the house, they went in.

The house was full of little people, young and old. There were women, men, and children. They had beautiful tables, and they were cooking all kinds of wild animal meat. Everyone was kind to the boy. They were glad to see him.

But the boy was careful. He saw squirrel meat on the table and said, "Little people, I want to take this!" And only then did he help himself.

On another table he saw raccoon meat. "Little people," he said, "I want to take this!" And again he helped himself.

When he had finished eating, they cleared off the scraps and put them into a barrel that was next to the fireplace. After a while, they took the lid off the barrel and a live squirrel came out.

They opened the barrel a second time and there was a live raccoon. Then they opened the door to the house, and the squirrel and the raccoon went out through the doorway.

After dinner the boy played with the other children and slept there that night. In the morning, when they had breakfast, the little man got ready to take the boy home. Again they went into the river and along the creek until they came to the path through the woods.

"Follow the trail across that ridge and it will take you straight home," said the little man. Then he returned to the river, and the boy kept on until he came in sight of his house.

A great many people were there, and when they saw him they ran up to him shouting, "There he is! He is not drowned or killed in the mountains!" They told him they had been hunting for him ever since sundown the day before and asked him where he had been.

"A little man took me to his house under the river," said the boy, "and the little people gave me a good dinner."

Then his mother said, "You say you had dinner?"

"Yes, and I had plenty, too."

"There is no house there," said his mother, "only the river." Then she laughed.

But those who know say that anyone who goes to the river on a warm summer day when the wind ripples the surface of the water—and listens carefully—can hear the little people talking below.

The Boy Who
Married the Little Woman

Maliseet NEW BRUNSWICK

There were two young boys whose father abandoned them, and as soon as they knew he had gone for good, their mother announced that she, too, couldn't stay at home anymore, and scarcely had she said the words than she disappeared.

When their food ran out, the children tracked their mother to a distant village. At the outermost house they stopped to ask directions. Woodchuck opened the door, and, seeing two strangers, she let out a cry.

Then the chief of the village said to his wife, "Strangers must have come. I hear Woodchuck crying."

Now, the wife of the chief was none other than the boys' own mother, who had come to the village a few days before, had quickly married, and was now living comfortably. Knowing that the strangers must be her sons, the cruel mother said to the chief, "Send Raven to get rid of them."

Raven was sent immediately. He went straight to Woodchuck's house, but when he saw the two boys he took a liking to them. Instead of getting rid of them, he brought them home to his own house and told his wife he wanted to adopt them, for Raven and his wife had no children. Then they began thinking how they could keep the two boys without the chief's knowing it. They decided to make two birch-bark boxes, and when that was done, they put a boy inside each box.

Raven lived a considerable distance from the chief's house, so the chief could not easily find out about the boys. Raven fed the boys well, and every night you could hear the boxes crack and creak as the boys grew. Raven was kept quite busy making new boxes for them.

After a while the boys grew too large to be recognized, and Raven threw the boxes away. Even their own mother, when she happened to see them, did not realize who they were. They were no longer the young children she had once known.

A trail led by the house. Raven had warned the boys not to use this path. But they paid no attention to him. One day they took some dried moose meat to keep from getting hungry, and off they went.

They traveled along a rocky trail and kept on that way for several days. Every day the trail grew smaller. Still they did not come to any camps or rivers.

On the seventh day, as it began to grow dark, they lay down to sleep, and while they slept the older boy had a dream. He saw a fire that kept moving toward him, and every time it came close he would take out his knife and stab it. Then the fire would die down again.

When he woke up, his brother was not there. The younger boy had gotten up early and had gone back to Raven's house. The older brother kept on, following the narrow trail, until at last he came to the seashore.

Beside the water he found a hollow log. He crawled into it and closed up the end. He floated around for a long time. When he realized that he had stopped moving, he opened the end of the log and looked out.

A surprise! There before him was a crowd of little people playing on the shore. When he called out to them, they ran and jumped into the sea. He wanted very much to catch one of them. So he dug a hole in the sand, crawled in, and covered himself up.

Soon the little people came out and started to play again. After a while they were right on top of him. Then he jumped up and seized one.

He said to the little man he had caught, "Now I have you, and you will have to stay with me and keep me company."

"That isn't possible," said the little man. "But I'll go get my sister. She'll keep you company and be your wife."

The boy hesitated, thinking he would never see the little man again, or his sister. But when the little man offered to leave his belt behind, the boy said he could go, and in a very short while the little man returned with his sister. Then he left again, taking his belt. From that moment the boy and the sister were married.

Then the boy started home with his little wife. When night came they put up a brush lodge. While the boy was out collecting firewood, the little woman hid behind one of the poles. When her husband returned, he was terribly disappointed not to find her. But when she saw how sad he was, it pleased her, and she came out from her hiding place.

During the long day's journey the boy had not been able to kill any game, and now he was hungry. He had said nothing about this to his wife, but she knew what was troubling him and said, "We'll soon have supper."

She put a grain of corn and a crumb of dried moose meat into a tiny bark pot with some water and put the pot over the fire to boil. The boy thought to himself, "What use will that little bit of meat be to me?"

She knew what he was thinking and said, "Don't worry. There will be enough for both of us."

When the food was cooked and they began to eat, there was more than enough. Every night after that the little wife did the same as she had done the first night, and the bit of dried meat lasted until they got back to Raven's house.

From then on, the little woman always cooked in this way—so that when she began to bake bread out of snow, nobody thought anything of it.

Well, that's the story.

Two Bad Friends

Inuit GREENLAND

A widow and her son lived by themselves in a winter camp, and just to the south lived another widow, who also had an only son. The two young men were friends. Every day they went out in their kayaks together, and always they kept each other company.

But one clear morning the young man who lived to the north woke up early and, feeling a light breeze from the east, called out to his mother, "Let me have my boots!" She threw them to him, saying, "Fetch me a skin for my bed in return!" and when he'd pulled on the boots, he jumped into his kayak and paddled off while his friend was still asleep.

He had not gone far, however, when suddenly he heard a noise from the sunny side of the bay. He turned around, and there was his friend with an angry face.

In the friend's hand was a harpoon aimed directly at him. As the harpoon came flying through the air, the one who had set out early turned himself over, kayak and all, and the weapon just touched the edge of the kayak and fell splashing into the water. Then he used his paddle to turn himself right side up again.

After that, the friend simply coiled up his harpoon line, and without ever mentioning what had happened, the two young men continued in their kayaks side by side, catching their seals and talking in a friendly manner on the way home.

"Just look," said the one. "The seaweed seems to be drifting landward."

"We'll soon have a storm," said the other. "Let's hurry to shore."

Time passed, and again the young man who had gone off by himself left home without waiting for his friend—who again slept late. And the same thing happened as before.

A third time it happened. And now at last the

one who was being attacked decided to take revenge: as soon as he rose up out of the water, after overturning his kayak as he had done the first two times, he aimed his own harpoon at his friend.

The friend, likewise, saved himself by turning over. But before he was able to get his kayak right side up again, his attacker was on top of him, and as he kept him under he said to himself, "He surely sleeps now."

After causing his friend to drown in this manner, or so he believed, the young man rowed toward land. The offshore islands were straight ahead. Yet before he could reach them, he noticed water coming into his kayak. He paddled as quickly as possible. But it was no use. He was already sinking. Then, fortunately, he remembered that the little people were his guardian spirits.

With a whispered cry of "Who comes to me?" he sent out his appeal for help. No sooner had he spoken than three little men came toward him in their small kayaks. Two of them held out paddles to keep him from sinking, while the third mended his leaking boat with a wad of blubber and handed him dry clothes to put on.

The little men had been out hunting seals, and

now they took all the seals they had caught and strung them together in a long line, telling the young man to tug them along so that he would have to row more strongly and would get warm that way. Then he paddled in front, while the others followed close behind.

After a while they came to a high island where a single house could be seen some distance up from the shore. A few moments later a shout came from within the house: "Come ahead. You are invited to step inside!"

Soon there were haulers running down to the shore carrying hauling-thongs decorated with fittings of bright walrus bone. Crying "Haul away!" they gathered the seals onto the beach. And as soon as the kayakers themselves had landed, they all went directly up the slope and into the house. When everyone had found a seat, the visitor looked around and noticed a little old man who seemed to be the master. His hair was as white as the side of an iceberg.

The old man returned the visitor's glance, then scolded the others. "Why weren't you quicker in helping him? Why did you let him get so cold?"

"He was already cold when he asked for our

help," said the others. "We came as soon as he called."

Then the old man gave the order "Let meat be brought for the stranger!" And when all had eaten their fill, and still there was more food, the old man looked out the window and said, "Go call our relatives." Immediately someone went out, and before long five other little men arrived.

Since no other house seemed near, the visitor who had been saved thought to himself, "Where can they be coming from?" More surprising still, they brought with them a young man just like himself—none other than his old companion, who he thought had drowned in his kayak. The lost companion, no longer lost, took a seat across from his friend and hardly dared look up.

When the newcomers had finished their meal, one of the hosts brought out a skin, spread it on the floor, and challenged his housemates and relatives to an arm-wrestling contest. But none were able to hold their own against him, nor were the two former friends who had come as visitors. All had to give in.

Overcome and put to shame, the visitors prepared to leave. But before they set out, the little

people scolded them sharply for their behavior and told them to give up their quarreling and be friends again.

On the way home, paddling their kayaks, the two began speaking to each other at last. The one who supposedly had drowned explained that he was restored to life just as his friend had been, by little kayakers arriving with dry clothes. It so happened that both young men were gifted with spirit power, and both had the little people as their guardian helpers.

"It's not easy to find someone to keep company with," said the one.

"Yes," said the other, "please stay and live with me."

From that time on, the two were friends. They never quarreled again.

The Little People
Who Built the Temples

Maya YUCATÁN

There was once a time when things happened in the best way possible, because the people who lived on earth had great knowledge. Their bodies were small, but their minds were large. They knew many secrets; they knew how to command water, wind, and everything seen or unseen.

This was the time when the temples were built and the stone roads that are still seen today. Whenever the little people wanted to make buildings, they just whistled, and the stones, even the very heavy ones, fell into place by themselves. The same was true of firewood. The little ones only had to whistle, and the wood would come by itself and fall onto the hearth.

In those days just one grain of corn was enough to feed a family for a day. And no one ever cut trees to clear a cornfield. They just whistled and the earth was ready to be sown with seed. These and many other things were known by the little people.

The work of the little people was done in darkness, before there was sun in the world. In those days the stones were soft and could be cut like wood. But as soon as the sun appeared for the first time, the stones became hard. From the time of that first morning, it became difficult to cut stone and to build.

And that's why today, when a man's house is still not finished after a long time building, the old people say, "It has become morning for him."

How the Dead Came Back

In the days when people were satisfied to cure sickness with roots and tree bark, that's when the medicine was pure. Even so, people died, and they had to go west to the Dark Land.

But any who were dead stayed away for just seven days. After that they'd come back to life.

It was the little people who brought them home. They'd get themselves a black box and start off from the east where the sun comes up and go out west to the Dark Land. Just two of the little people would be sent. One would carry the front end of the box, and the other would carry the back end.

One time it was a young girl who had died, and

two of the little ones set off with their black box to bring her back.

Before they left they were each given a short stick of sourwood, and this is what they were told: All the dead people would be at a circle dance, and the two little ones would have to stand outside the circle. When the girl passed by, they'd have to touch her with their sticks and she'd fall to the ground. Then they'd put her into the black box and carry her off. But they had to be sure not to open the box, not even a little, till they were all the way home.

So they took the sticks and the box, and they walked seven days, and they crossed seven ridges of mountains, till they got to the place where the sun goes down. Many people were there, and they were all having a circle dance, exactly the way the little ones had been told.

The young girl who had recently died was in the outside circle, and as she swung around to where the little people were standing, they touched her with their sourwood sticks, and she fell down. Then they put her into the box and closed the lid. The other ghosts never seemed to notice what had happened.

Then they sealed the box tight, so there was no air in it and no cracks.

On the way back the little people rested at the first mountain ridge. At the second ridge they rested again, and there they heard the young girl ask for just a little hole in the box to breathe through. They said no.

They traveled on to the third ridge, and the fourth, and the fifth, and the sixth. And each time they rested. When they got to the seventh ridge, they rested again. But this time one of the two had to step away for a moment, and as soon as the one was out of sight, the other made a hole in the box so the poor girl could breathe, and just as the hole was opened a strong wind blew out.

When they got back home and took the lid off, the box was empty.

If the little people had kept the box closed, as they'd been told to do, they would have brought that young girl home safely, and we today would be able to bring our friends back from the Dark Land. Now, when they die, we cannot bring them back.

Except for doctors. Doctors remember when the little people could still bring you home, and if

somebody is sick, the doctor can say these magic words:

> They did it then,
> we'll do it now.
> The two went out,
> those little ones—
> from sunup,
> came to sundown,
> found her dead,
> carried her off,
> made her alive.

If the cure works, the person gets up and feels well. In the ancient days, they say, the little people were powerful.

The Little Man
Who Married the Whirlwind

Seneca NEW YORK

In the days when the little people lived everywhere and the whirlwinds still had their nests in the tops of the tallest pines, there was a little uncle who lived with his nephew, and they kept a house by themselves in a deep forest.

One morning the nephew, all out of breath, ran into the lodge crying, "Oh, uncle, I have heard something wonderful, singing *dee dee dee*."

"Oh!" said the uncle. "That is the bird called chickadee. It is the first kind of game a young hunter shoots." Then the little nephew reached for his bow and arrows and ran out the door. When he returned with a tiny bird, the uncle dressed it and hung it on the cross stick to broil, saying, "Now my nephew will become a great hunter."

As he grew older, the little nephew hunted larger game, and finally he was old enough to bring home a deer. "My nephew, I am pleased with you," said the old uncle one evening. "You are now a little man and may go hunting in any direction you like. Except east. You must never go east."

The next morning the little man started off, going directly south. But as soon as he was out of his uncle's sight he turned and went east. He kept going for some time, until he came to a place where the trees had been cleared. By chance he looked up, and at the far edge of the clearing he saw a woman sitting on a log.

She called out to him, "Come here and rest. I know you are tired."

At first he paid no attention to her. But when she had called to him a third time, he went and sat on the end of the log. "Why do you sit so far away?" she asked. "Don't young people usually sit closer when they talk?"

The little man drew nearer and finally took his

seat right at her side. "You must rest your head in my lap," she said. In her mind she was thinking, "This little man is as fine-looking and handsome as I want a man to be."

Then she began to tell stories, talking on until at last, growing drowsy, the little man fell asleep. When she could hear that he was sleeping soundly, she put him into her pack basket and hurried away through the air.

After a while she stopped and said to her little passenger in a loud voice, "Wake up!" Both his arms flew out, and he opened his eyes. "Do you know this place?" she asked.

"Oh yes," he said. "I have hunted here many times with my uncle."

Then she was satisfied, saying to herself, "He travels far in his hunting."

She kept on, moving through the forest with the speed of the wind. Late in the afternoon she stopped at a lake. Putting down the basket, she said to the little man, "Do you know this lake?"

His arms trembled for a moment, and he opened his eyes. "Oh yes," he replied, "I have fished here many times with my uncle."

Again she was satisfied, saying to herself, "He

travels far in his fishing. He provides well."

Searching in her basket, she found a tiny canoe the size of a walnut. She struck it with her hand repeatedly until it became large enough to hold both herself and the little man. Then the little man knew that the woman had magic power—for she was one of the whirlwinds.

They got into the canoe and paddled across the lake. "We are almost there," she said. "I have a mother and three married sisters. We all live together in my mother's lodge with my sisters' three husbands. You and I will live with them."

They traveled on until they reached the lodge. As they stood at the door, the mother cried, "Welcome, son-in-law. I am glad you have come. Now let us see if I will have dreams."

And with that the little man became the daughter's husband. But at night, when all had retired, his wife said to him secretly, "My mother will try to kill you by testing your power."

That night the old woman had a strong dream. It was so strong it tossed her from side to side, and she fell off her sleeping platform and rolled across the floor to the edge of the fire.

"Oh, what a dream I have had!" she cried. "My

Dream Spirit tells me my son-in-law must kill the Great Bear and must return to this lodge before the door flap stops swinging." But in her heart she was saying, "The Great Bear will put an end to my son-in-law."

To this the little man said nothing but "Oh, I will take care of that in the morning, for small as I am, I am the strongest man under the blue sky."

And when daylight came, he ran out of the lodge with the door flap swinging and split a hickory tree from top to bottom, taking half to make a bow and half to push the sun back toward the east. Then he ran through the dark forest, tracking the bear. "I can smell it!" he cried. Then: "Here it is!"

Using pine trees for arrows, he brought the bear to the ground. As it fell, its body crushed the forest with a great cracking sound. The sun was just coming up again, and the door flap was still swinging, as he dragged the Great Bear to the front of the lodge.

The next night the old woman dreamed again. This time her Dream Spirit told her that her son-in-law must make a feast and invite the whirlwinds. For she was the mother of all the whirlwinds in the world, and she demanded that her daughter's husband feed them. But in her heart she was thinking, "The food will run short. The whirlwinds will eat him, too."

The day after that, the little man went into the forest before the sun was up, and when he returned, he was bringing elk, deer, moose, and other game. Then he went to the lakes and the rivers and brought home fish, until at last the heap of food was touching the lowest clouds.

When all was ready, the little man called to the whirlwinds, "Come eat your fill!"

From their nests in the tops of pine trees all over the world each one answered, "I am coming!"

And at that moment, far off in the deep forest, the little uncle heard the voices and thought to himself, "My little nephew is coming at last," and he shaded his eyes with his hands and began to watch. But when no one came to him, he gave up all his hoping, put out his fire, and scattered the ashes on his head in sadness.

On the other side of the forest the whirlwinds had already begun to appear. They came in great numbers, and before long the seats, the shelves,

and even the floor of the mother-in-law's lodge were filled with their huge round heads. They started to eat, and they ate with a terrible appetite. The old woman went around urging them, "Eat, eat! Eat your fill!"

The little man's wife, her three sisters, and their three husbands kept going outside and bringing in more. Finally the whirlwinds had eaten until they could eat no more. "Mother, we have eaten enough!"

At this the little son-in-law began to dance around the outside of the lodge, singing:

> let this lodge
> be hard as flint
>
> let it be red hot
> let it be white hot

Then the walls and roof became white hot, and the whirlwinds and the whirlwind mother-in-law flew round and round, knocking the sides of the lodge and making such a noise as had never been heard in the world before. When the lodge was in flames, the great heads burst, and their spirits flew up through the smoke hole and out into the air.

"Let all their trails disappear!" cried the son-in-law, and at last there was nothing but ashes.

Then the little man with his wife and her three sisters and all their husbands set out for the house in the deep forest where the little man's uncle lived. They went by the same road the wife had traveled before.

When they came to the shore of the lake, the wife once again took a tiny canoe from her basket and struck it with her hand until it became large. Then every one of them got into the canoe, and they paddled across the water.

Reaching the far shore, they continued on until they were almost to the lodge of the little man's uncle. From a distance they could hear him weeping, "Ten summers I will mourn for him."

The little nephew called out, "Oh, Uncle, I have returned." But the uncle did not believe it and made the little man thrust his arm through a hole in the door flap. Then the uncle caught the scent and knew at once it was his own flesh and blood. "Oh, Nephew! Wait a moment until I clean up."

Quickly the uncle brushed the ashes out of his

hair and smoothed the skins on his sleeping platform. When all was ready, he threw open the door
flap and welcomed the nephew, his wife, her three
sisters, and the sisters' three husbands.

And there at the lodge of the little uncle they
lived on. They had plenty to eat and lived well.

Now then, that's the story.

The Rainmakers' Apprentice

Nahua MEXICO

Once long ago a boy named José stumbled into a mountain cave, not knowing it belonged to the little rainmakers. Inside the cave were the rainmakers' gardens, where flowers grew year-round and vegetables were always ripening. The rainmakers adopted José and made him their gardener.

One day the rainmakers went traveling. José was left by himself.

In the corner of the cave stood three barrels that José had been told he must never touch. But this time José's curiosity got the best of him, and he lifted the lid off one of the barrels. The moment it was opened, there was thunder.

Then he lifted the lid off the second barrel, and rain began to pour. As he opened the third barrel, lightning flashed.

Such a terrible storm happens only when one of the rainmakers' helpers opens up barrels while the rainmakers themselves are off in the sky trying to direct the rain.

When the little rainmakers came home, they told José he would have to leave. Then they sent him back to his people. But in spite of his bad behavior, they did favors for him the rest of his life.

Whenever there was drought, the little rainmakers brought rain and made it fall on José's cornfield. They did not forget him, and through the years his crops were always green.

Thunder's Two Sisters

Cherokee NORTH CAROLINA

Years ago the people used to have many more dances than they do today. They had a dance every week.

One night, after the dance was well started, two young women with beautiful long hair came in. They danced with one partner and then another. No one knew who the beautiful strangers were or where they had come from.

One of the young men was attracted to the older of the two sisters. But when the sisters left the dance, and he tried to follow them, they slipped away.

Seven nights later they came again to the dance.

Again the young man followed them, and again they slipped away. Then the young man went to a doctor and asked for attraction medicine. The doctor told him to bathe in running water and gave him words to say.

The following week on the day of the dance the young man went to the stream just at daybreak, washed himself as he had been told, and said the words:

> Your soul
> Has come into the very center
> Of my soul,
> Never to turn away.

That evening the two sisters came again. This time, when they left to go home, the young man was able to follow them.

As they walked along, the older sister turned around and asked, "Which one of us did you wish to speak to?" But she already knew his thoughts, and from that moment the young man and the older sister were married.

They began to climb, following the bed of a stream that flowed down the mountain. After a

while they heard drumming in the distance, and the higher they climbed, the louder it grew.

At last they reached a hole in the rocks where the stream came out from inside the mountain. "This is where we live," said the sisters.

They went in, and the hole became wider and wider until it opened into a large cave filled with hundreds of little people, drumming and dancing inside the mountain. Water was dripping from the roof of the cave.

There were young people, and infants in their mothers' arms, and old men with white beards that hung to their knees. "Let me be like this!" said the younger sister, and at that moment she became small.

"Let me be like this!" said the older sister, and she too became small. Then she sat down and invited the young man to join her. "Here, sit beside me," she said.

But when he tried to sit down, he felt the seat moving beneath him. He looked again and saw that the seat was a turtle with its head sticking out of the shell. It reached toward him with its claws, and he jumped.

"I can't sit here," he cried. "It's a turtle!"

"No, it's only a seat," she insisted.

The drumming was getting louder. Then a roll of thunder was heard.

"That must be our brother," said the sisters. "He's one of the Thunders." And as they spoke, a little man came riding into the cave on the back of a huge rattlesnake. Every time the rattlesnake's tongue darted out there was lightning.

"You can help us with our work," said the little man to his new brother-in-law. "Here, saddle up and let's ride!"

The older sister brought in a second rattlesnake, and the younger sister said, "Here! Here's the saddle!" But the saddle was another turtle.

The young man began to tremble. With one hand he tried to steady himself against the wall of the cave, and in that moment the sisters and their brother knew he was afraid.

Suddenly everything disappeared, and the young man was standing with his feet in the rocky stream, holding on to a laurel bush that grew from the bank. Slowly he made his way down the mountain and reached his own settlement. He had been gone so long, people thought he had died. Yet to him it seemed only the day after the dance.

If he had not been afraid, he would have been happily married. If he had been more daring, he would be up in the sky world today, riding with the little Thunders.

The Smallest Bow

Seneca NEW YORK

At the edge of a clearing in a thick pine forest an old woman and her grandson lived together in a bark lodge. All the other members of the family had died. Only the grandmother and the boy remained.

One day the grandmother took from the wall a bow that was grimed with smoke. She cleaned it carefully and handed it to the boy, saying, "This was your uncle's bow. We will make a trial at shooting."

They stepped outside, and the old woman pointed to a tree and told the boy to take aim. Without waiting to be asked twice, he strung an arrow and hit the tree, and the grandmother said to him, "That kind of shooting will do. You must now begin hunting."

The next morning, starting out early, the grandson went to the woods and shot birds, putting many together on a string. When he returned at noon, his grandmother greeted him at the door with the words "I thank you, Grandson. We are well-off now and will have plenty."

Then she took the birds, dressed them, and cooked them with boiled corn. As soon as the dish was ready, they sat down and ate, while the grandmother continued praising her grandson.

The morning after that the boy went out again, walking toward the river. The air was misty, but he could hear paddling and the soft sounds of a canoe's approach. A moment later the canoe landed, and two little men got out.

They came to where the boy was standing and stopped directly in front of him. Each one had a tiny bow and a quiver of arrows, much smaller than the boy's own bow and arrows. "We came on purpose to talk to you," said one of the little men, "for we know that you get up early."

Then the other one asked this question: "How would you like to trade your bow and arrows for

one of our bows and a set of our arrows?''

"I can't do that," said the boy. "Yours are much smaller than mine."

Then one of the little men put a string on his tiny bow and, taking an arrow, shot it straight up. The arrow disappeared into the sky and never came down at all. Then he said to the boy, "You may be right. Your bow may be bigger. But the great things on earth are not always the biggest. You may live to learn that."

Without further words the two little men took up their canoe paddles, and with one stroke the canoe shot into the air, sailing over the woods and under the clouds.

Too surprised to say anything, the boy went home to his grandmother and told her all that had happened.

Then the grandmother scolded her grandson, saying, "You made a mistake by not trading with the little people. If you had taken their bow and arrows, you could have hunted down any game you wanted. Those little bows are magic. From now on, never be too hasty in judging people as you see them, for you never know who they are or what they may be."

The Little Woman
Who Taught Pottery

Toba ARGENTINA

There was a very, very little old woman, not much taller than a child of five. She was the one who taught us to make pots. Her name was Kopilitára.

Before she taught others, she tried it herself. When she had made the first pot out of clay, she dug a hole in the ground and built a fire. Then she fired the pot to harden it.

When the pot was well fired, she took wild-orange seeds, put them in, and left them to boil. After a while she tasted them and saw that they were good. She told the people, "If you need pots, I can teach you to make them."

Many women came to be taught. And in this way our ancestors learned to make pottery.

Those who were learning tried to pay for their lessons. They offered presents to Kopilitára. But she refused. She told them she needed nothing, she wanted nothing. It was her pleasure to cook and make pots.

And when she made pots, she gave them away. If someone needed a bowl to serve mush, the little old woman would make it and fire it.

And so the people were able to get cooked food whenever they needed it. The little old woman gave pots and bowls to everyone who asked.

How the Dark Dance Began

Seneca NEW YORK

It's a story very old and known only by few. My father used to tell it when we were small.

Long ago there was a boy named Snow, who lived with his family along the bank of a river. While he was still young, he obeyed his parents and did not chase birds that flew toward the south—where he had been told he must never go.

But one morning, when he had grown a little older, he took up his bow and arrows and began to hunt cedar waxwings. It was spring and there were many of these birds in the tall trees. Just as he was about to shoot, the birds flew toward the south. They kept on flying up the bed of a stream that branched off the main river. Snow ran after them.

As he was chasing the birds, he noticed cliffs on either side of the stream rising higher and higher. As he followed on, the light became dimmer. It grew dark, and he could hardly tell where to walk among the jagged rocks.

Suddenly he heard a small stone strike the ground at his feet. Then another stone struck him on the forehead between the eyes, and Snow fell over like a dead person.

After a long time he heard voices. They were talking about him, and he heard someone say, "Now we have him."

He kept his eyes shut, waiting for a chance to escape. Everywhere were footfalls and small voices. Finally he made up his mind that there was nothing dangerous in the sounds he could hear, and he opened his eyes.

On all sides were little people, dressed in clothing like his own. There was a shout when he looked around him, and he was told to rise and be seated. He could now see clearly by the light of the fire that the little people had lit on the rocky bottom of the gorge.

Along the stone walls on either side were clay

pots, baskets, tiny tubs of strawberries, and bundles of spicebush twigs. Some of the little people were warming themselves at the fire, while others were making strawberry soup.

When the soup was ready, the headwoman in charge came over to where Snow was sitting and said, "We have lived in this place from the beginning, and we were put here to help your people. But you did not know us. Now that you have come, we will celebrate with our ceremony. It's called Dark Dance. You must learn it and carry it back to your people."

Then the headwoman picked up a water drum and gave three taps with a tiny drumstick. It was not long before little people from everywhere began coming in. When all had arrived, the headwoman instructed one of the grandfathers to give the Opening Speech. Then the grandfather spoke these words:

> You who run in the darkness,
> You, the little people,
> You are the wanderers of the mountains,
> You have promised to hear whenever the
>   drum sounds,
> Even as far away as a seven days' journey.

As soon as the speech was finished, strawberry soup was served in little bowls, and when everyone had tasted it, the headwoman covered the fire and there was darkness. Snow sat next to the old man, who now began drumming and singing. All the rest joined in and continued until the old man gave one beat of the drum, and the singing was over.

After a rest, there was singing again, then two more rests, each followed by singing. Snow listened and learned the songs.

When morning came, the old man told the boy he must now go home and teach the ceremony. "It will be the connecting link between your people and the little people," he said, "and it will bring you luck."

"May you have good dreams," said the boy as he started for home.

"May you have good dreams," replied the old man. And when he had finished speaking, he and all the rest disappeared, and the boy found himself in the place where he had met the little people the day before, at the bottom of the cliffs.

When Snow finally reached home, his family and friends were relieved to have him back, and all said, "Thanks." Then he taught them the Dark Dance, which must always be performed at night in a darkened room, and this is the ceremony that has come down to the present day.

When the little people hear the drum, they arrive quickly, even from great distances. Their voices can be heard singing with the others, but in the darkness no one sees them.

The Hunter
Who Lost His Luck

Seneca/Cayuga NEW YORK AND ONTARIO

In the ancient days, it is said, there lived a good mother and her son in a lodge that stood alone. Since the son was a hunter who always came home with game, the mother's storage sacks overflowed with smoked meat, and her sleeping platforms were piled with rare, excellent furs.

The young man soon caught the attention of mothers who had marriageable daughters, and one by one the young women were instructed to make loaves of marriage bread. Then each would arrive at the young man's lodge with the bread and a firm proposal. "Indeed," the young woman would say, "I believe you and I should marry."

To this the hunter would always reply, "It is my settled purpose not to marry." And having failed, the young woman would return to her home. Many times the young man's mother scolded him. "If you don't marry," she warned, "you may have bad luck. You may find yourself with a snake on your hands."

When autumn came the young hunter went deeper into the forest than usual, and when he was seen again he was bringing deer meat and bear meat and many kinds of skins. Then people from everywhere came to his lodge, each with something of value to trade.

One brought a bracelet, saying, "For this cut me off a small portion of bear meat."

Another brought a beaded sash, saying, "For this give me the skin of a beaver, for I have come to buy." The trading continued for some time, and all kept saying of the young man, "He is protected from bad luck."

One night, as the young hunter was just falling asleep, a little woman appeared before him. She was neatly dressed and good-looking. The young man spoke to her and was pleased when she said she would stay and be his wife.

The next night she came again, and the following day the young man was unable to go out and hunt, for he could do nothing but think of the little woman.

His mother saw that something was on his mind and thought she would find out what it might be. When night came she stayed awake and listened, and after a while she heard talking.

The little woman, aware that she was being overheard, said to the hunter, "Your mother wishes to see me in the morning."

Early the next day, when the young woman went out, the old mother followed her and saw that she was one of the little people. She was pleased that her son had at last found a wife and said to herself, "I am thankful."

When the little woman came back, she brought a corn pounder, also berries and dried corn. At once she began to cook food. She had with her a little pot for boiling the berries, and she also made corn bread in very tiny cakes.

"That may not be enough to fill us up," said the young man. But the little woman laughed and said, "You will see when it's cooked."

As soon as the meal was ready, they all sat down.

Then each took a spoonful of berries and some of the bread. "See if you can eat a whole corn cake," said the little woman. But when they tried, they were unable to finish. Just a tiny piece filled them up.

From then on, the young man found that he could kill game more easily. The neighbors, too, had better luck, and all were greatly pleased.

But each time the young husband set out to hunt, his wife would give him this warning, "When strangers come up to you, don't speak to them." Again she would tell him, "If someone calls to you, don't answer."

As it happened, when he went to the woods he would often hear someone whistle. Sometimes a strange woman would be there. But he would always keep his distance.

One day, after traveling a long while, he came to a swamp and started to walk around it. All at once he heard a whistle and saw a woman standing on a log. She was well dressed and had long hair beautifully arranged on her head. Her face was painted, and the young man instantly took a liking to her.

Suddenly the strange woman threw her arms

around the young hunter's neck, and in that moment he lost consciousness. The following morning, long after daybreak, he finally awoke. As he
set out for home, he felt changed, as though he
had lost his senses. When he reached the lodge,
his wife was gone.

From that day on, his luck was bad. Again and
again he tried to hunt but could find nothing.

After many days he thought of the woman in the
woods and decided to look for her. When he
reached the place where they had met before, he
saw only a snake. It made a noise that sounded as
if it were laughing.

The young man returned to his lodge and sat in
silence. His mother questioned him, but he made
no answer. He seemed not to hear her.

By this time the neighbors, too, were having bad
luck and could not find game. Finally the little
woman reappeared. "You didn't do as I told you,"
she said, and she let him know that she had seen
what had happened. "From now on, your luck will
always be bad," she said, "and you will never again
find bear or deer." Then she disappeared for the
last time.

Again the young man tried his hand at hunting.

But he could not approach the game. He would see animals at a distance, but they would run off before he could come near. The same was true for his neighbors.

After that, there was never another chance for the young hunter and his neighbors to marry one of the little people. It never happened again—and it may never yet, though I think most likely they are still hoping.

Star Husbands

Passamaquoddy MAINE

One day it happened to Marten as it might have happened to anyone. He came to a lake far off in the mountains—and as Marten always did, he approached softly, walking like a cat.

Behind a rock were grapevines. He heard laughter. Young women were there. They were swinging from vines, jumping into the lake, splashing in the water.

The young women were little people, and the little people always avoid being seen. Yet Marten, who was gifted with magic, spied on them and chose the one he liked best.

Then he saw that their clothes were lying on the bank. Quietly he crept up, as Marten always does—

no one saw him—and he took the clothes in his hands. Now, if a man steals the clothes of little people, he is able to catch them, because their power is in their clothes.

And that's what Marten did—he stole the clothes. Then he ran along the shore, shouting. When the little women saw him, they were furious and ran after him, and the one he desired most was the first to catch up with him.

As soon as she was within touching distance, Marten tapped her very lightly on the head. And at just that touch they were married.

Astonished to be married so suddenly, the little woman fainted. Gently Marten carried her off, after giving back the others their clothes.

Now, Moose, finding out that Marten was married, came to visit and heard the tale. He said to himself, "This sounds easy; it's not hard at all. I'm starting to feel married already."

So he went to the lake in the mountains and found the rock where the grapevines hung low. He saw the little women jumping and splashing, playing in the water like mad fishes. He became excited, stole all the clothes, and started to run off.

The little women were close behind him, and

the one he most wanted was the one who caught up with him first. He knew what to do: He picked up a club and hit her on the head as hard as he could. Immediately she fell dead.

So Moose was not married.

Then Marten and his wife lived on for a while, until one day the little wife decided she would go home and visit her people. But Marten said he himself would go instead and would come back with one of her sisters. That way, he thought, he would have two wives instead of one, and his wife would have company.

So again Marten went to the lake, to the rock where the grapevines were, and again he captured one of the little people. He carried her off, and just with that the two were married.

Then Moose was more dissatisfied than ever. He told Marten he would have to give him one of his wives. Marten said no.

Moose begged. Marten refused.

Moose kept insisting that Marten give him a wife or go back to the lake and get him a wife or find him a wife somewhere else, and in a fury he picked up a huge club and chased after Marten.

From then on, the two were enemies.

Now, Marten was cleverer than Moose and had a way of getting even—he made flint-headed arrows and shot them at Moose's head. After that, things were worse than ever. Every evening they would make new weapons, and in the morning they would use them against each other.

Disgusted, the two little women made up their minds to leave. And so, one morning while Moose and Marten were trying to kill each other, the two little wives ran away. All day they ran, and at nightfall they stopped to rest.

Now, it happens at sunset that the voice of the wind is heard from far off. The moon rises into the sky, and there's loneliness over the land. Lying on the ground in an oak opening, deep in the woods, the two little women looked up at the stars and made wishes. One said to the other, "If those stars were men, which would you marry? I'll take the one with the twinkling red light."

The other replied, "I like the bigger stars. I'll take that yellow one."

They were only pretending. Or so they thought. The next morning when they awoke, they found themselves married again—in the usual way, at only a touch.

The one who had wished for the bright yellow star opened her eyes, and there was her husband, a handsome man. The one who had mentioned the red star woke up and saw the very one she had wanted, a little man with a twinkling in his eyes.

As they desire, so they receive.

The Twelve Little Women

Lenape NEW YORK

In the cliffs at the mouth of the Delaware River, on the right bank, were four openings, or caves, leading to a house inside the rocks where twelve little women lived. People used to bring articles of value and leave them for safekeeping in these caves.

When any man passed by on the river, the little women would come out and ask where the man came from, where he was headed, and how his crops were growing. If they received a kind answer, they let him go on with good wishes. They were satisfied.

If he was impudent in his answers, they immediately ran down to the river and chased him. And if they caught him, they plucked every hair from his body except the hair of his head.

If they were unable to catch him, they called on their uncle, a great serpent, who lived in a deep hole in the ocean outside the mouth of the river. Their uncle would come at once, raise his head above the water, and draw a breath that would sweep the man into his mouth.

All the older and better people gave kind answers to the little women, but younger and thoughtless men were sometimes insolent.

One day a young man was passing by, and the twelve little women asked him where he was going. "I won't tell you," he said. Then they started after him, and when they caught him, they pulled out all the hair but the hair of his head and sent him home bleeding.

When he got back home, he went to the chief and complained, "Why do we have such women? Let's drive them away. Let's send them to some other nation."

"Oh, never mind," said the chief. "They don't hurt good people. Let them stay where they are."

So matters went on. All good-minded people

gave kind answers to the little women, had good luck, and went on their way undisturbed, while others were plucked, or swallowed by the serpent.

From the hair that they collected, the little women wove bags and took them to the deep water where fish were caught. They would ask each fisherman for something to put in their bags, and no matter how many fish the man had in his canoe, the little bags could hold them all and were never full.

If the fisherman gave his fish willingly, he would later catch so many that he wouldn't know what to do with them. If he grumbled, he caught no more and had bad luck.

When the twelve little women went home and emptied their bags, the fish that had become so small that thousands of them would fill a little bag regained their natural size and were just as large as they had been before.

One time a number of young men were insolent to the little women and went home all bleeding from the loss of their hair. They began to complain, and the other young men said, "We must get rid of these women. They cause too much trouble."

Just then, one of them said, "I can put an end to them all by myself."

So the next day he passed by the caves and was insolent to the little women. They chased him all over the flats opposite their caves. But they couldn't catch him. Then they called on their uncle, who rose out of the water and began to draw in his breath.

The young man was willing to be swallowed by the serpent. And letting himself be carried by the current, he went into the huge open mouth. Inside the serpent it was like a great room. Its ribs were like planks in a house.

With his flint knife the man made a cut between two ribs and sliced his way out. Then he ran around behind the rocks where the little women had their house.

When they saw that the serpent was wounded, the women began to cry and weep, saying, "Our uncle is dying! Our uncle is dying!" They hurried down to where he lay and continued to groan and cry till he died.

While they were crying, the young man went into their house, where he found a great quantity of bear's oil; and taking dry weeds, he piled them up in all the rooms, poured oil on them, and set fire to everything. In no time the whole place was burning.

The little women, seeing their house in flames, ran home and began to make water on the fire.

But it was no use. Everything burned. The walls fell in, and the house itself was completely destroyed except the four entrances.

By this time a great many people had gathered on the far bank of the river, looking up at the cliff where the fire was burning.

From the top of the cliff the little women called down to them and said, "If you had left us in peace, we would have taught you many things, taught you all the things those strangers know who live on the other side of the ocean.

"A hundred years from now they will come here and drive you away, and you will have no land.

"You will be poor, no people.

"This is what will come to you for driving us away."

After that they disappeared. And no one knows to what place they went.

The Talking Tree

Yaqui MEXICO

In the ancient time, when the country was wild, there lived a small people called Surem. In those days there were huge turtles living in the river and in the sea—and large animals everywhere, on the land and in the water.

From the ground to the sky stretched an enormous tree that talked, making a humming noise like bees. The talk was telling the Surem and all the animals how to live. It said that some of the animals would get their food by hunting, others by eating grass. And it told the little Surem how the Conquest would come, and how there would be a new religion and new laws.

The Surem, although they were small, had power. But they did not like the thought of new laws and of strangers coming, and when they heard the tree, some of them went into the earth, to live inside of hills. Others went to live in the sea.

The few who remained on the surface of the earth grew taller than the other Surem and became the people of today.

The Surem of the ancient time were a little people, but they were strong. Today they still live underground and in the sea. Some say the Surem are rich and have many cattle under the hills.

The Surem favor the earth-surface people and help them whenever they can. They warn boats when danger is near. Or, if people are lost in the desert, the little Surem take care of them by bringing them food and fire.

When the danger is past, the Surem disappear. But they always return if someone is in need.

The Talking Tree ᴥ *113*

The Deetkatoo

There was a woman whose husband stopped liking her. They had two small children, a girl and a boy. The man left his wife, and he left his children, too. These were poor people.

The woman stayed with her two married brothers. They lived together. The brothers fished. The woman herself went every day to dig fern roots. Day after day she went.

Sometimes she would go all day without eating. Sometimes she would leave early in the morning and return at noon.

One day it happened that every time she threw out dirt from where she was digging, something would cry. She looked and looked. "I can't see what it is that's crying," she said to herself.

She went home without finding out. The next day she made up her mind to look more carefully. She ate no food that morning, then hurried off and dug in the same place as before.

Again, each time she threw out dirt, something cried. After a while she began to watch the spot where she was throwing the dirt. And there he was. She saw him.

She had heard what to do with a Deetkatoo if you found one. She thought, "I wonder if he is willing for me to have him?" She picked the little person up, took off her wrap, and wrapped him in it. Then she dug a hole in the sand and put him there. She covered it all over and laid sticks and leaves on top. Then she gathered up her fern roots and went home.

When she got home, she laid her pack of roots outside the door, went in, and went to bed. She said to her daughter, "Tell your aunt to fix those roots for the rest of you to eat. I don't feel well."

The next morning the woman would not get up from her bed. She seemed to be sick. Her brothers worried over her, "Do you want a doctor?"

She answered, "No, I do not want a doctor."

"Do you feel very sick?" they asked.

"No, not very sick."

The third day she got up early. Then she went out and looked at the Deetkatoo. Already his hair was turning into shell money. She went home, sat by the fire awhile, then went to bed again. She did not eat. Two more days she stayed in bed.

The fifth morning she got up and went to look at the little man again. He had now turned almost entirely into shell money.

The woman's brothers began to realize that their sister's strange behavior must have something to do with a power of some kind. So they let her alone. It took ten days of fasting for that Deetkatoo to turn completely into money.

On the tenth day the woman got up and went out again, taking her soft rush basket with her. Oh! That Deetkatoo was all turned into money beads. The head had turned into buffalo-horn dishes, beautifully carved. The eyes had turned into two very large beads. She gathered all the wealth and put it into her soft rush basket. She came home with her basket quite full and put it in her bed.

Her sisters-in-law wondered, "What can she have in there?" And now that her fast was over, she asked for food, and they fed her.

Then she sorted her shell money into lengths. She made strings of it. Strings of short beads she gave to her sisters-in-law, strings of long ones she gave to her brothers. Some of the shell money she kept for herself. She made a headdress, breastplate, and earrings for her little girl, and she put earrings on her boy.

The children went out to play. They were extremely happy. People began to notice them. They said, "Why, those children never had anything like that before. Now they are all dressed up so nicely. They have money beads to wear and earrings."

Everybody was talking. And in this way the woman's husband finally heard about it and walked around in that direction. He asked his children, "Who gave you those things?"

The girl answered, "No one gave them to me. My mother made them for me."

Then the husband thought to himself, "There might be something worth coming home to." He returned to his wife. She explained to him everything that had happened, and after that he stayed around. After that, he treated his wife and his children very well.

That is all.

Guide to Tribes and Cultures

Two of the great language families of Native America—the Algonquian and the Iroquoian—account for more than half the stories in this book. Among the other families represented are the Guaicurúan (of South America), the Uto-Aztecan (of western North America and Central America), and the Eskimo-Aleut (of the far north). The notes that follow indicate how the different languages (and the tribes or cultures for which they are named) relate to one another through these family groups.

AZTEC, *see* Nahua.

CAYUGA, *see* Iroquois.

CHEROKEE. An Iroquoian people prominent in the history of Georgia, Tennessee, and the Carolinas until forcibly removed to Oklahoma by the United States government in 1838–39. Now divided between eastern Oklahoma and the Smoky Mountain region of western North Carolina.

INUIT (IN-oo-it). Also known as Eskimo, the world's northernmost people, native to Greenland, Canada, Alaska, and eastern Siberia. The Inuit are native American but not American Indian. They speak languages related to Aleut, spoken in the Aleutian Islands (off the coast of southwestern Alaska). The story "Weaker and Weaker" is from Baffin Island, a part of Canada just west of Greenland.

IROQUOIS (pronounced EAR-ah-kwoy in the United States, EAR-ah-kwah in Canada). Iroquois is the general name for the well-known Six Nations—Mohawk, Oneida, Onondaga, Cayuga, Seneca, and Tuscarora—of New York and Canada. The Iroquois are related by language to the Huron (of Quebec) and the Cherokee.

LENAPE (luh-NAH-pay). An Algonquian people, also known as the Delaware. Of the two principal divisions, the Munsee Delaware, now mostly in Ontario (but with descendants also in western New York, Wisconsin, and elsewhere), were formerly in what is now the New York City metropolitan area. The U-nami Delaware, now mostly in Oklahoma, were originally in the Philadelphia area and southern New Jersey. "The Twelve Little Women" is from the Munsee.

MALISEET, *see* Passamaquoddy.

MAYA. The Maya family includes most of the languages spoken in Guatemala and southeastern Mexico, including Maya proper, or Yucatec, the native language of the Yucatán Peninsula. The Tzotzil (tzoat-SEAL) of Chiapas State, southern Mexico, are another of the Maya groups, all of whom are related to the ancient Maya whose great civilization during the period A.D. 300–900 produced the temples and pyramids for which the Maya are renowned.

MOHAWK, *see* Iroquois.

NAHUA (NAH-wuh). A group of closely related peoples of central Mexico, speaking varieties of Nahuatl, a Uto-Aztecan language. The Nahua are descended from the ancient Aztecs, whose empire (stretching from central Mexico to the Guatemala border) fell to Spanish conquerors in 1521. The Yaqui (YAH-kee), another of the Uto-Aztecan groups, live in northwest Mexico, with additional communities (dating from the 1930s) in southern Arizona. The Yaqui, who defended their territory until 1887, were among the last of the native peoples of Mexico to come under the authority of the Mexican government.

PASSAMAQUODDY. An Algonquian people of the state of Maine. The Passamaquoddy are closely related to the Maliseet, who live mostly across the Canadian border in the province of New Brunswick. Passamaquoddy speakers can understand Maliseet, and vice versa.

SENECA, *see* Iroquois.

TILLAMOOK. A people of coastal Oregon, speaking the south-ernmost language of the Salishan family (which includes the Bella Coola of British Columbia, the Lummi of Washington, the Flathead of Montana, and many others). *See* Yurok, below.

TZOTZIL, *see* Maya.

TOBA. A native people of Paraguay and Argentina, whose lan-guage, also called Toba, is a member of the Guaicurúan family (which formerly had speakers throughout a large region ex-tending from southern Brazil to northern Argentina and as far west as the Andes Mountains). The Toba live in the so-called Gran Chaco, a famously difficult habitat of alternating grass-lands and scrub woodland, dry in the winter, excessively hot and partly flooded during the rainy summer.

YAQUI, *see* Nahua.

YUROK. A small nation of the northern California coast, whose language is distantly related to the Algonquian family of eastern and central North America. Culturally, however, the Yurok of traditional days—with their wooden houses and shell-money economy—were comparable to the Tillamook and other Northwest Coast tribes.

ZUNI (ZOO-nee). A people of western New Mexico, whose language is not clearly related to any other. Culturally the Zuni are related to the Hopi, the Taos, and other town-dwelling, or Pueblo, groups of the Southwest.

Guide to the Lore of Little People

One of the pleasures in hearing Native American folktales about little people is in recognizing familiar themes and details that belong especially to them. The following outline is designed to reveal at a glance how six key topics (Food, Rain, Helpfulness, Unkindness, Home Life, and Personal Traits) are presented in the stories. A closer look shows which stories are the sources in each case.

Food

Little people have sacks of food: Weaker and Weaker, All Are My Friends, The Twelve Little Women
    use magic cooking pots: Three Wishes, The Boy Who Married the Little Woman, The Hunter Who Lost His Luck

bake magic bread:
　　from snow: The Boy Who Married the Little Woman
　　from corn: The Hunter Who Lost His Luck
can make a grain of corn last all day: The Little People
Who Built the Temples

Rain

Little people command rain, thunder, and lightning: The
Rainmakers' Apprentice, Thunder's Two Sisters
　　command water and wind: The Little People Who Built
　　the Temples
　　command wind: Proud-Woman and All-Kinds-of-Trees
　　live at Thunder Mountain: The Little Ones and Their
　　Mouse Helpers

Helpfulness

Little people extend hospitality: Three Wishes, Proud-Woman
and All-Kinds-of-Trees, The Girl Who Married the Little
Man, The Little House in the Deep Water, Two Bad Friends,
How the Dark Dance Began
　　have generous feelings toward all: All Are My Friends, The
　　Little Woman Who Taught Pottery, How the Dark Dance
　　Began, The Talking Tree
　　give willingly if permission is asked: The Little House in
　　the Deep Water
　　bring luck: Three Wishes, Proud-Woman and All-Kinds-

of-Trees, How the Dark Dance Began, The Hunter Who Lost His Luck, The Twelve Little Women, The Deetkatoo
have power to cure illness: How the Dead Came Back, How the Dark Dance Began
serve as guardian spirits: Two Bad Friends
promote respect for others: Three Wishes, Two Bad Friends
throw stones to make contact: The Little House in the Deep Water, How the Dark Dance Began
come when called: Two Bad Friends, How the Dark Dance Began

Unkindness

Little people tease others: Proud-Woman and All-Kinds-of-Trees, The Boy Who Married the Little Woman
    punish others with bad luck: The Hunter Who Lost His Luck, The Twelve Little Women

Home Life

Little people live in the earth:
    in rocks: Three Wishes
    in rocky gorges: How the Dark Dance Began
    in hills: The Talking Tree
    in caves: The Rainmakers' Apprentice, Thunder's Two Sisters, The Twelve Little Women
  live in water:

in streams or rivers: The Little House in the Deep Water, Thunder's Two Sisters

in lakes: Star Husbands

in the sea: The Boy Who Married the Little Woman, The Talking Tree

live in the woods: Proud-Woman and All-Kinds-of-Trees, The Little Man Who Married the Whirlwind, The Deetkatoo

live in large groups (or have relatives): The Girl Who Married the Little Man, The Little House in the Deep Water, The Boy Who Married the Little Woman, The Rainmakers' Apprentice, Thunder's Two Sisters, How the Dark Dance Began, The Twelve Little Women

avoid being seen: The Girl Who Married the Little Man, How the Dark Dance Began, Star Husbands, The Deetkatoo

protect the secret of where they live: Three Wishes

are in danger of being captured: Proud-Woman and All-Kinds-of-Trees, The Boy Who Married the Little Woman, Star Husbands

Personal Traits

Little people have long hair: The Little House in the Deep Water, Thunder's Two Sisters

are very old:

    with white hair: Two Bad Friends

    with white beards: Thunder's Two Sisters

have wisdom: The Little People Who Built the Temples

have great strength: Two Bad Friends, The Little Man Who Married the Whirlwind, The Talking Tree

are playful: The Boy Who Married the Little Woman, Star Husbands

are gifted with extrasensory perception: The Little House in the Deep Water, The Boy Who Married the Little Woman, Thunder's Two Sisters, The Smallest Bow, The Hunter Who Lost His Luck

can change size: Thunder's Two Sisters

Notes

Sources here cited by author or by author and short title are fully listed in the References.

Introduction

Page ix / Diminutive figures dating from the Olmec: Wauchope, vol. 3, pp. 755–56, and vol. 11, p. 739; Covarrubias, figs. 11 and 12. *Page ix* / Maya figures: Miller and Taube, p. 82; J. E. S. Thompson, p. 341. *Page x* / Little people as helpers of the rain god: Garibay, p. 26. *Page x* / Story of Food Mountain: Bierhorst, *History*, p. 147. *Page x* / Story of a foolish king: ibid., pp. 156–57. *Page xi* / Little people at Chichén Itzá and Uxmal: J. E. S. Thompson, pp. 340–41; Redfield and Villa, pp. 330–31. *Page xii* / World will be entirely changed: Laughlin, p. 77. *Page xii* / Pipil lore: Schultze Jena, pp. 27–32. *Page xii* / Yaqui lore: see "The Talking Tree," this volume. *Page xiv* / South American pygmies: Wilbert, pp. 8–15. *Page xiv* / Court dwarfs: Torquemada, vol. I, p. 298 (bk. 3, ch. 25); Schele and Miller, pp. II, 122, 130, 150. *Page xiv* / Yupa lore: Wilbert, pp. 86–89. *Page xiv* / Aztec legend of dwarfs who froze: Sahagún, bk. 3, p. 35; cf. Spence, p. 141. *Page xv* / Cherokee stories: Reed. *Page xvii* / Inuit spirit helpers: Boas, *Central*, p. 183; Thalbitzer, vol. 2, pp. 248–78; Rink, p. 39. *Page xviii* / Little people as source of power among Cherokee: Mooney, "Sacred Formulas," p. 341; Kilpatrick and Kilpatrick, *Walk* and *Run*. *Page xviii* / "I am to fail in nothing!": Kilpatrick and Kilpatrick, *Walk*, p. 49. *Page xviii* / "You will be holding my soul": Kilpatrick and Kilpatrick, *Run*, p. 133. *Page xviii* / Dark Dance: Parker, *Code*, p. 119; Wilson, pp. 203–12. *Page xix* / Nahua ritual: Sandstrom, pp. 249–50, 300. *Page xix* / Iroquois thunderer: Curtin and Hewitt, "Seneca Fiction," p. 456. *Page xix* / Cherokee "thunders": Kilpatrick and Kilpatrick, *Friends*; Mooney, "Myths," p. 248. *Page xx* / Little brothers live on Thunder Mountain: Cushing, *Zuñi Folk Tales*, p. 175, and *Zuñi Breadstuff*, pp. 383, 632. *Page xxi* / Zuni war god statues: Suro; Anyon. *Page xxi* / Little people and the Trail of Tears: Lombardi, p. 38. *Page xxii* / "The eternal ones" . . . present when the world was created: Kilpatrick and Kilpatrick, *Friends*, pp. 81, 191; Mooney, "Myths," p. 253. *Page xxii* / First person to be seen after the world had been made: Fenton, p. 97. *Page xxii* / Oonabgemesuk: Leland, p. 18. *Page xxii* / Tzotzil lore: Laughlin, p. 77.

Stories

Page 3 / Weaker and Weaker. Adapted from Boas, *The Eskimo of Baffin Island and Hudson Bay*, pp. 202–3. Details from ibid., pp. 173, 190, 215, 220, 236, 251, 255, 302, 311.

This little tale comes from Cumberland Sound on the east coast of Baffin Island, about fifty miles south of the Arctic Circle. It was collected in the late 1800s by Franz Boas, who was the first outsider to make a careful record of Inuit life in northeastern Canada.

In the old days the usual Inuit house was a one-room dome-shaped structure, or igloo, with a tunnel-like passageway at the entrance. In some cases, as here, there might be a second, smaller room to one side of the main room. Along the walls of either room were raised benches, or sleeping platforms, usually with partitions for privacy.

Page 7 / Three Wishes. Adapted from Horne et al., pp. 160–70.

Told in the Mohawk language, the story text uses the term *iakotinenióia'ks* ("stone throwers"), here translated "little people." The Native name comes from the belief that the little people announce themselves by throwing stones—though they do not do so in the present story. The teller is Josephine Horne; the collector is the linguist Marianne (Williams) Mithun.

Page 12 / Proud-Woman and All-Kinds-of-Trees. Adapted from Curtin and Hewitt, "Seneca Fiction," pp. 452–53. Details from ibid., pp. 155, 162, 188, 207, 401, 418, 463, 555, 577, 586, 629; Parker, *Seneca Myths*, pp. 74, 205, 208, 274.

In traditional Seneca society, marriages were arranged by mothers or other female relatives, and it was the young woman herself who took the initiative by bringing loaves of bread to the young man who had been selected. In old-style stories, as here, this important gift is referred to as "marriage bread."

Page 18 / The Girl Who Married the Little Man. Adapted from Rink, pp. 183–86.

According to Henry Rink, the pioneering collector of Greenlandic lore, the little people were "a sort of elves or gnomes, supposed to have their abodes within rocks along the seashore." *Atliarusek* and *ingnersuak* are two Native names for these diminutive folk encountered in old tales from western Greenland.

In the story, the boat used by the little people is an umiak, a large rowboat capable of carrying several passengers. The somewhat smaller kayak held only one person, typically a seal hunter.

Page 25 / The Little Ones and Their Mouse Helpers. Adapted from Cushing, *Zuñi Folk Tales,* pp. 104–27. Details from Benedict, vol. 2, pp. 153–54, 198; Cushing, *Zuñi Breadstuff,* pp. 271, 277, 429.

The story of the twin brothers' courtship is one of their milder adventures. In other tales the mischievous "little ones" turn children into birds, torment their poor grandmother, slay dangerous monsters, or acquire rainmaking power by stealing thunder and lightning (Benedict, vol. 2, pp. 285–95).

Like all Zuni folktales, "The Little Ones and Their Mouse Helpers" takes place in the old time, when the Zuni still lived in apartment houses made of stone. Since the typical "door" was an opening in the roof, people entered by climbing a ladder to the roof, then climbing *down* a second ladder into the house.

Page 32 / All Are My Friends. Adapted from Kroeber, pp. 116–23.

The little man called Megwomets is one of the Yurok "immortals," who lived during the myth age, planned the earth, established customs, then disappeared. This account of Megwomets, given by the Yurok storyteller Lame Billy of Weitspus, was recorded in the early years of the twentieth century by the great student of California Indian culture Alfred Kroeber.

Page 35 / The Little House in the Deep Water. Adapted from Mooney, "Myths," pp. 331–32. Details from ibid., pp. 331, 336, 345–46, 476; Witthoft and Hadlock, p. 415; Kilpatrick and Kilpatrick, *Friends,* pp. 80–81, 86.

Among the Cherokee, stories about the little people are by no means a thing of the past, nor are they regarded as strictly fictional. The tale of the little house in the deep water is typical of the older stories, in which the little folk are usually helpful. The more recent accounts emphasize their troublesomeness (Reed; Lombardi; Witthoft and Hadlock, pp. 414–16; Fogelson, p. 92).

Page 41 / The Boy Who Married the Little Woman. Adapted from Mechling, pp. 50–55.

The little man's belt, which ensures his return, recalls the Old World motif catalogued by the folklorist Stith Thompson as F451.3.1: *Power of dwarf in his belt.* "Star Husbands" (see note, below) is another story in which the power of little people is said to be in their clothing.

Page 48 / Two Bad Friends. Adapted from Rink, pp. 358–61. Details from ibid., pp. 96, 111, 155, 159, 160, 163, 178; Thalbitzer, vol. 2, p. 264.

Among the Inuit of the old time, it was essential for a hunter to have a special friend who could help out in time of need. But as countless stories attest, such close, constant friendships sometimes turned sour. In this tale, at least, the little people are able to set things right.

As suggested by the story, the kayak is a one-person boat with a watertight cover, or deck. Sitting snugly in a hole in the deck and wearing a waterproof jacket attached to the rim of the hole, the rider propels the kayak using a double-bladed paddle. Even if overturned, the watertight boat can be righted without danger of sinking.

Page 55 / The Little People Who Built the Temples. Adapted from Redfield and Villa, pp. 330–31; Tozzer, p. 153.

A Maya story of this sort is called an *ejemplo*, a term borrowed from Spanish, meaning "example." It tells of happenings in a long-ago time but in a way that is applicable to the present.

The ancient "temples" of Yucatán undoubtedly served a variety of purposes. Some may have been used as ceremonial chambers, others as rulers' residences. The architecture includes terraces, courtyards, and pyramids surmounted by small chambers decorated with sculptured figures, as seen at Chichén Itzá, Uxmal, and other well-known sites.

Page 58 / How the Dead Came Back. Adapted from Kilpatrick and Kilpatrick, "Eastern Cherokee Folktales," pp. 388–89; Mooney, pp. 253–54.

The basic plot—coincidentally—is similar to the Greek myth of Orpheus, who tried unsuccessfully to bring his lost wife home from the underworld. Stories of this kind, therefore, are known to folklorists as Orpheus tales (Hultkranz). In the present version the role of Orpheus is played by two of the little people, trying to be helpful.

In former times the power of the little people was often invoked by traditional Cherokee doctors, who used spoken charms, or incantations, as well as medicinal herbs.

Page 63 / The Little Man Who Married the Whirlwind. Adapted from Curtin and Hewitt, "Seneca Fiction," pp. 84–86 and 422–28. Details from ibid., pp. 79, 107, 139, 186, 239, 352, 387, 403, 405–6, 408, 474, 490, 582, 753; Myrtle, p. 123.

Whirlwinds, also known as "flying heads," are standard characters in Seneca folklore. Bodiless and with long tangled hair, they sweep through the forest with terrifying speed. Sometimes they are friendly, however, and in a few cases they may take the form of an ordinary human being.

Page 73 / The Rainmakers' Apprentice. Adapted from Madsen, pp. 131–32.

The tale of the rain gods' disobedient helper, who unleashes a thunderstorm, is also told by the modern Maya of Yucatán and Guatemala (Bierhorst, *Monkey's Haircut*, pp. 66–71, 146). But although the Maya story is essentially the same as the tale told by the Nahua, the Maya rain gods, called Chacs, are not envisioned as little people.

Page 75 / Thunder's Two Sisters. Adapted from Kilpatrick and Kilpatrick, "Eastern Cherokee Folktales," pp. 392–93; Mooney, "Myths," pp. 345–47. Details from Witthoft and Hadlock, p. 419; Mooney, "Myths," pp. 240, 316, 328, 377; Mooney, "Sacred Formulas," p. 377; Kilpatrick and Kilpatrick, *Run*, p. 62; Kilpatrick and Kilpatrick, *Friends*, p. 89.

Some Cherokees have said that the Thunders belong to two separate classes: those that live in the far west above the sky and those that live in the mountains. The sky dwellers are supposed to be kind and helpful, while the mountain dwellers are always plotting mischief (Mooney, "Myths," p. 257). But in some stories, as here, the two traditions are combined, and it appears that the Thunders spend time in both locations.

Like the young hero of the story, Cherokee men in the old days could obtain love medicine from a traditional doctor, or shaman. Spoken words were often used. Ritual cleansing, known to the Cherokee as "going to the water," might also be recommended to ensure success (Kilpatrick and Kilpatrick, *Walk*, pp. 9–10).

Page 81 / The Smallest Bow. Adapted from Curtin and Hewitt, "Seneca Fiction," pp. 347–48, 401; Cornplanter, pp. 83–84. Details from Curtin and Hewitt, "Seneca Fiction," pp. 98, 162; Parker, *Seneca Myths*, pp. 97, 108; Smith, p. 19.

This seemingly simple story brings together three of the most important traits associated with little people: strength ("The arrow disappeared into the sky and never came down at all"), wisdom ("The great things on earth are not always the biggest"), and extrasensory perception ("We came on purpose to talk to you, for we know that you get up early").

Page 85 / The Little Woman Who Taught Pottery. Adapted from Métraux, p. 86.

Kopilitára (kaw-pee-lee-TAH-rah), who taught women to make pottery, is said to have had a little husband, Kosodót, who taught men to hunt (Métraux, p. 84–86). According to a somewhat different report, also from the Toba, the original pottery makers were a class of little women, called *waishí* (Wilbert and Simoneau, p. 187).

The wild orange *(naranja del monte),* also called *sachalimona* by the Toba, is *Capparis speciosa,* a staple food that can be dried and stored. The "mush," mentioned toward the end of the story, is made from the seeds of the carob tree, or algarroba, *Prosopis nigra* and *P. alba.* (Steward, vol. I, pp. 246, 263; Wilbert and Simoneau, p. 591).

Page 87 / How the Dark Dance Began. Adapted from Parker, *Seneca Myths,* pp. 331–33; Parker, *Code,* pp. 120–21; Cornplanter, pp. 46–57.

In his well-known description of the Dark Dance, originally published in *The New Yorker,* the literary critic Edmund Wilson writes of witnessing a performance held in western New York in January 1958. As Wilson and his companions were about to enter, "the darkened house in the snow seemed quite spooky. From within came the sound of singing, which, given its beat by the rattles and drums, pounded on, through episodic pauses, with a steady compelling rhythm."

The description continues: "At the first intermission, the lights were turned on, and we went in by the back door. We found ourselves in a very large kitchen, in which the singers and musicians and the audience were sitting along the walls, leaving the rest of the floor clear for the dancers. An immense boiler of soup was keeping hot on an old-fashioned wood stove" (Wilson, p. 204).

Page 93 / The Hunter Who Lost His Luck. Adapted from Curtin and Hewitt, "Seneca Fiction," pp. 555–64; Waugh, no. 58.

The story of the hunter whose wife brings him luck until he proves untrue to her is widespread in North America. Usually the wife is a buffalo (S. Thompson, *Tales*, no. 57) or a deer (Fisher, no. IX–9).

On "marriage bread," see the note to Proud-Woman and All-Kinds-of-Trees, above.

Page 100 / Star Husbands. Adapted from Prince, pp. 59–61.

The Native storyteller has here combined two of the best-known tale types of North American Indian lore: the so-called Swan Maidens (in which a young man steals the clothes of a beautiful young woman and makes her his bride) and the Star Husbands (in which two young women, climbing into the sky, become the wives of star men). Versions of both stories are told across the continent from the Pacific to the Atlantic (S. Thompson, *Tales*, pp. 330–31, 356).

Page 106 / The Twelve Little Women. Adapted from Bierhorst, *White Deer*, pp. 99–104 (as transcribed from the original text in Curtin and Hewitt, Seneca [and Delaware] myths).

Told in the late 1800s by John Armstrong, a member of the Lenape band of exiles that had settled among the Seneca of western New York, the story recalls the days when the Lenape had lived along the Delaware River in western New Jersey and eastern Pennsylvania.

Page 112 / The Talking Tree. Adapted from Giddings, pp. 25–27.

Although the Yaqui fought successfully to keep Mexicans out of their territory until 1887, they had been partially converted to Christianity by Jesuit missionaries who arrived in 1617. The "Conquest" mentioned in the story, therefore, refers to the early Jesuit period, when many Yaqui were baptized and the old Yaqui villages, or *rancherías,* were re-formed into Spanish-style towns (Spicer, p. 172; Sturtevant, vol. 10, pp. 250–63).

Page 114 / The Deetkatoo. Reprinted from Jacobs, pp. 165–67.

Among traditional Native Americans, fasting, or abstinence from food, is used as a prayer for success. Thus the woman in the story, seeing a chance to save herself from poverty, fasts for ten days—and is rewarded.

For the Tillamook and other tribes living along the coasts of Washington, Oregon, and California, seashells were the principal form of money. Especially prized were the tubular, slightly curved tusk shells, or dentalia. The longer the shell, the greater the value. Tillamook men wore a special tattoo on one arm for the purpose of measuring dentalia (Sturtevant, vol. 7, p. 562). We may understand, therefore, why the husband in the story was eager to return to his wife after hearing that she had acquired shell money.

References

The following list is highly selective, intended mainly to provide references for the Introduction and stories above. Native American little-people lore is scattered in hundreds of additional sources. The subject as a whole, however, has received little scholarly treatment. The single major work is Roth's compilation (see below). This and other works devoted exclusively to little people are here marked with an asterisk (*).

Anyon, Roger. "Zuni Repatriation of War Gods," *Cultural Survival Quarterly*, winter 1996 (vol. 19, issue 4), p. 47.

Benedict, Ruth. *Zuni Mythology*. 2 vols. New York: Columbia University Press, 1935.

Bierhorst, John. *History and Mythology of the Aztecs: The Codex Chimalpopoca*. Tucson: University of Arizona Press, 1992.

——. *The Monkey's Haircut and Other Stories Told by the Maya.* New York: Morrow, 1986.

——. *The White Deer and Other Stories Told by the Lenape.* New York: Morrow, 1995.

Boas, Franz. *The Central Eskimo.* Lincoln: University of Nebraska Press, 1964.

——. *The Eskimo of Baffin Land and Hudson Bay,* Bulletin of the American Museum of Natural History, vol. 15. 1907.

Cornplanter, Jesse J. *Legends of the Longhouse.* Port Washington, N.Y.: Ira J. Friedman/Kennikat Press, 1963. Originally published 1938 by J. B. Lippincott.

Covarrubias, Miguel. *Mexico South.* New York: Knopf, 1967.

Curtin, Jeremiah, and J. N. B. Hewitt. Seneca [and Delaware] myths. [1883–.] Mss. 3860, 5 boxes. National Anthropological Archives. Smithsonian Institution, Washington, D.C.

——. "Seneca Fiction," *Thirty-second Annual Report of the Bureau of American Ethnology, 1910–11,* pp. 37–813. Washington, 1918.

Cushing, Frank. *Zuñi Breadstuff.* New York: Museum of the American Indian, 1920.

——. *Zuñi Folk Tales.* Tucson: University of Arizona Press, 1988. Reprint of 1931 edition.

Fenton, William N. *The False Faces of the Iroquois.* Norman: University of Oklahoma Press, 1987.

Fisher, Margaret W. "The Mythology of the Northern and Northeastern Algonkians." In Frederick Johnson, ed., *Man in Northeastern North America,* Papers of the Robert S. Peabody Foundation for Archaeology, 3:226–62. Andover, Mass.: Phillips Academy, 1946.

*Fogelson, Raymond D. "Cherokee Little People Reconsidered," *Journal of Cherokee Studies*, fall 1982, pp. 92–98.

Garibay K., Angel M. *Teogonia e historia de los Mexicanos.* 3rd ed. Mexico: Porrúa, 1979.

Giddings, Ruth. *Yaqui Myths and Legends.* Anthropological Papers of the University of Arizona, no. 2. Tucson, 1959. Reissued by University of Arizona Press.

Horne, Josephine, et al. *Kanien'kéha' Okara'shón:'a:: Mohawk Stories* (ed. Marianne Williams). New York State Museum Bulletin 427. Albany, 1976.

Hultkranz, Ake. *The North American Indian Orpheus Tradition.* Statens Etnografiska Museum Monograph Series, no. 2. Stockholm, 1957.

Jacobs, Elizabeth Derr. *Nehalem Tillamook Tales* (ed. Melville Jacobs). University of Oregon Monographs, Studies in Anthropology no. 5. Eugene: University of Oregon Books, 1959.

Kilpatrick, Jack Frederick, and Anna Gritts Kilpatrick. "Eastern Cherokee Folktales." *Anthropological Papers.* Bureau of American Ethnology, Bulletin 196. Washington: Smithsonian Institution, 1967.

———. *Friends of Thunder.* Dallas: Southern Methodist University Press, 1964.

———. *Run Toward the Nightland.* Dallas: Southern Methodist University Press, 1967.

———. *Walk in Your Soul.* Dallas: Southern Methodist University Press, 1965.

Kroeber, A. L. *Yurok Myths.* Berkeley: University of California Press, 1976.

Laughlin, Robert M. *Of Cabbages and Kings: Tales from Zinacantán*, Smithsonian Contributions to Anthropology, no. 23. Washington, 1977.

Leland, Charles G. *Algonquin Legends*. New York: Dover, 1992. Originally published 1884 by Houghton Mifflin.

*Lombardi, Betty J. "Comments on the Little People Stories Collected from the Cherokee Indians of Northeastern Oklahoma," *Mid-America Folklore* 12(1): 32–39. 1984.

Madsen, William. *The Virgin's Children: Life in an Aztec Village Today.* Austin: University of Texas Press, 1960.

Mechling, W. H. *Malecite Tales.* Canada, Department of Mines. Geological Survey, Memoir 49. Anthropological Series, no. 4. Ottawa, 1914.

Métraux, Alfred. *Myths of the Toba and Pilagá Indians of the Gran Chaco.* Memoirs of the American Folklore Society, vol. 40. Philadelphia, 1946.

Miller, Mary, and Karl Taube. *The Gods and Symbols of Ancient Mexico and the Maya.* London: Thames and Hudson, 1993.

Mooney, James. "Myths of the Cherokee," *Nineteenth Annual Report of the Bureau of American Ethnology, 1897–1898*, pt. I, pp. 3–548. Washington, 1900.

———. "The Sacred Formulas of the Cherokees," *Seventh Annual Report of the Bureau of American Ethnology, 1885–1886*, pp. 301–97. Washington, 1891.

Myrtle, Minnie. *The Iroquois.* New York: Appleton, 1855.

Parker, Arthur C. *The Code of Handsome Lake.* New York State Museum Bulletin 163. Albany, 1913.

———. *Seneca Myths and Folk Tales.* Buffalo: Buffalo Historical Society, 1923.

Prince, John Dyneley. *Passamaquoddy Texts.* Publications of the American Ethnological Society, vol. 10. 1921.

Redfield, Robert, and Alfonso Villa R[ojas]. *Chan Kom: A Maya Village.* Washington, D.C.: Carnegie Institution of Washington, 1934.

*Reed, Jeannie, ed. *Stories of the Yunwi Tsunsdi: The Cherokee Little People.* A Western Carolina University English 102 Class Project, March 1991. Includes 78 newly recorded stories.

Rink, Henry. *Tales and Traditions of the Eskimo.* Edinburgh and London: Blackwood, 1875.

*Roth, John E. *American Elves: An Encyclopedia of Little People from the Lore of 340 Ethnic Groups of the Western Hemisphere.* Jefferson, N.C.: McFarland, 1997.

Sahagún, Bernardino de. *Florentine Codex: General History of the Things of New Spain* (ed. Arthur J. O. Anderson and Charles E. Dibble). Parts 1–13 (introductory volume and books 1–12). 1st ed, 1950–82. Books 1–3 and 12, 2d ed., rev., 1970–81. Santa Fe, New Mexico: School of American Research and University of Utah Press.

Sandstrom, Alan R. *Corn Is Our Blood.* Norman: University of Oklahoma Press, 1991.

Schele, Linda, and Mary Ellen Miller. *The Blood of Kings: Dynasty and Ritual in Maya Art.* New York and Fort Worth: George Braziller / Kimbell Art Museum, 1986.

Schultze Jena, Leonhard. *Indiana,* vol. 2: Mythen in der Muttersprache der Pipil von Izalco in El Salvador. Jena, Germany: Gustav Fischer, 1935.

Smith, Erminnie A. *Myths of the Iroquois.* Ohsweken, Ontario: Iroqrafts, 1983. Reprint of 1883 edition.

Spence, Lewis. *The Gods of Mexico.* New York: Stokes, 1923.

Spicer, Edward H. *The Yaquis: A Cultural History.* Tucson: University of Arizona Press, 1980.

Steward, Julian H., ed. *Handbook of South American Indians,* 7 vols. Bureau of American Ethnology, Bulletin 143. Washington, 1946–59.

Sturtevant, William C., ed. *Handbook of North American Indians,* vols. 4–11, 15, 17. Washington, D.C.: Smithsonian Institution, 1978–96.

Suro, Robert. "Quiet Effort to Regain Idols May Alter Views of Indian Art," *The New York Times,* Aug. 13, 1990, pp. A1, A13.

Thalbitzer, William. *The Ammassalik Eskimo.* 2 vols. (*Meddelelser om Grønland* 39–40 and 53). Copenhagen, 1914–41.

Thompson, J. Eric S. *Maya History and Religion.* Norman: University of Oklahoma Press, 1970.

Thompson, Stith. *Motif-Index of Folk Literature,* 6 vols. Bloomington: Indiana University Press, 1955–58.

———. *Tales of the North American Indians.* Bloomington: Indiana University Press, 1966. Originally published 1929.

Torquemada, Juan de. *Monarquía indiana.* 3 vols. Mexico: Porrúa, 1975. Reprint of the 1723 ed.

Tozzer, Alfred M. *A Comparative Study of the Mayas and the Lacandones.* New York: Macmillan, 1907.

Wauchope, Robert, ed. *Handbook of Middle American Indians.* 16 vols. Austin: University of Texas Press, 1964–76.

Waugh, F. W. Collection of Iroquois Folklore. Typescript. Canadian Ethnology Service, National Museums of Canada. Hull, Quebec.

Wilbert, Johannes. *Yupa Folktales.* Los Angeles: UCLA Latin American Center, 1974.

Wilbert, Johannes, and Karin Simoneau, eds. *Folk Literature of the Toba Indians,* vol. 1. Los Angeles: UCLA Latin American Center, 1982.

Wilson, Edmund. *Apologies to the Iroquois.* New York: Random House / Vintage, n.d.

*Witthoft, John, and Wendell S. Hadlock. "Cherokee-Iroquois Little People," *Journal of American Folklore* 59(1946): 413–22.

John Bierhorst is the author/editor/translator of many books on Native American lore, including *In the Trail of the Wind: American Indian Poems and Ritual Orations; A Cry From the Earth: Music of the North American Indians; Spirit Child;* and *The Naked Bear: Folktales of the Iroquois*—all of which were named Notable Books by the American Library Association.

o ———————————————————————————————— o

Ron Hilbert Coy, a member of the Tulalip tribe of western Washington, is a painter, illustrator, and sculptor whose works are in the collections of the Seattle Arts Commission, the Bureau of Indian Affairs, and other institutions. He has written that his personal goal is "to enhance individual minds with my people's way of life and culture."